Candy had wanted that kiss from the moment Jake strolled through the door on Monday afternoon

She suspected it had something to do with that sexy grin, maybe a little more with his delicious masculine scent. But more and more she was suspecting it was the way he cared for baby Bonnie. Walking in on the two of them sleeping in that recliner flip-flopped her heart in a thousand tiny ways.

For all these years, she'd blamed him for breaking her heart, but had he been the one responsible? Or had she done the breaking all by herself?

Because as tough as Jake came across on the outside, those moments when she caught him smoothing Bonnie's hair, fixing the collars on one of her tiny dresses or planting a kiss on top of her head, spoke louder than any words he ever could have spoken. Jake was no heartbreaker, for in taking orphaned Bonnie into his home and arms he was a *heart mender*.

Dear Reader,

What a spectacular lineup of love stories Harlequin American Romance has for you this month as we continue to celebrate our 20th anniversary. Start off with another wonderful title in Cathy Gillen Thacker's DEVERAUX LEGACY series, *Taking Over the Tycoon*. Sexy millionaire Connor Templeton is used to getting whatever—whomever—he wants! But has he finally met his match in one beguiling single mother?

Next, *Fortune's Twins* by Kara Lennox is the latest installment in the MILLIONAIRE, MONTANA continuity series. In this book, a night of passion leaves a "Main Street Millionaire" expecting twins—and has the whole town wondering "Who's the daddy?" After catching a bridal bouquet and opening an heirloom hope chest, a shy virgin dreams about asking her secret crush to father the baby she yearns for, in *Have Bouquet, Need Boyfriend*, part of Rita Herron's HARTWELL HOPE CHESTS series. And don't miss *Inherited: One Baby!* by Laura Marie Altom, in which a handsome bachelor must convince his ex-wife to remarry him in order to keep custody of the adorable orphaned baby left in his care.

Enjoy this month's offerings, and be sure to return each and every month to Harlequin American Romance!

Melissa Jeglinski
Associate Senior Editor
Harlequin American Romance

INHERITED: ONE BABY!

Laura Marie Altom

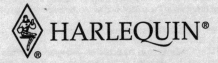

HARLEQUIN®

TORONTO • NEW YORK • LONDON
AMSTERDAM • PARIS • SYDNEY • HAMBURG
STOCKHOLM • ATHENS • TOKYO • MILAN • MADRID
PRAGUE • WARSAW • BUDAPEST • AUCKLAND

This one's for grandparents. Those I dearly miss:
Joe and Lu Jachim, Shirley Jeanne Alisch and Doris Altom.
And those I'm still fortunate enough to have with me:
Fred Alisch, Sylvia Altom-Shelton and my honorary
grandparents, Katie and Paul Sage.
I love you all very much.

ISBN 0-373-16976-0

INHERITED: ONE BABY!

Copyright © 2003 by Laura Marie Altom.

This edition published by arrangement with Harlequin Books S.A.

® and TM are trademarks of the publisher. Trademarks indicated with ® are registered in the United States Patent and Trademark Office, the Canadian Trade Marks Office and in other countries.

Visit us at www.eHarlequin.com

Printed in U.S.A.

ABOUT THE AUTHOR

After college (Go Hogs!), Laura Marie Altom did a brief stint as an interior designer before becoming a stay-at-home mom to boy/girl twins. Always an avid romance reader, Laura knew it was time to try her hand at writing when she found herself replotting the afternoon soaps. She has written three romances for another publisher.

When not immersed in her next story, Laura enjoys a glamorous lifestyle of lounging by a pool that's always in need of cleaning, zipping around in a convertible while trying to keep her dog from leaping out and she is constantly striving to reach the bottom of the laundry basket—a feat she may never accomplish! For real fun, Laura's content to read, do needlepoint and cuddle with her handsome hubby.

Laura loves hearing from readers at either P.O. Box 2074, Tulsa, OK 74101, or via e-mail: BaliPalm@aol.com.

Books by Laura Marie Altom

HARLEQUIN AMERICAN ROMANCE
940—BLIND LUCK BRIDE
976—INHERITED: ONE BABY!

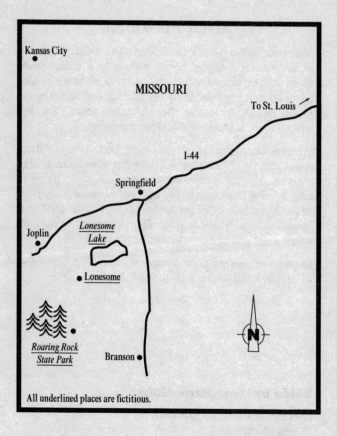

KANSAS CITY

MISSOURI

To St. Louis

I-44

Springfield

Joplin

Lonesome Lake

Lonesome

Roaring Rock State Park

Branson

N

All underlined places are fictitious.

Prologue

"Come again?" Jake Peterson said to the silver-haired dynamo in charge of his infant daughter's adoption case. The metal desk she sat at had probably once been painted a color, but over the years it had become a crazy quilt of smiling faces. Children's faces captured in photos. Hundreds of them—maybe even thousands. Mrs. Starling had made all of these children happy. Why couldn't she do the same for his baby girl?

"You're telling me that just because this Elizabeth Mannford is related by blood to Bonnie that that makes her a better parent? Having me raise their daughter was my friends' dying wish. You can't take Bonnie away from me—the only family she knows!"

"Mr. Peterson, please, there's no need for raised voices. Butterscotch?" She gestured toward a lumpy clay dish brimming with gold-wrapped candies. "I find butterscotch to be the most soothing of flavors, don't you?"

Jake hardened his jaw.

He didn't want to come down on this grandma. Really, he didn't, but what else could he do?

He wouldn't break his promise to Cal and Jenny who had been killed six weeks earlier by a drunk driver. He wouldn't lose this chance in a million to make good on a dream he'd long since had for himself. The dream to somehow, some way become a father—just as long as that way didn't include having a wife.

"Look," he said, taking a calming breath. "I love Bonnie. And as CEO of Galaxy Sports, I make much more than an adequate living."

"Miss Manning doesn't dispute either of those things."

"Then what's her problem? Why is she doing this?"

"In a nutshell," Mrs. Starling said, lacing her fingers atop a stack of manila folders. "After speaking with her at length this past Tuesday, it's my opinion that she's just plain lonely. Bitter about the way her life has turned out...and is now wanting to make amends, but not quite sure how to best go about it.

"From what you've told me about her relationship within her great-niece's family, she was an outcast. The black sheep, if you will. Her niece, Jenny, was all she had left in the world—and, of course, Bonnie. As such, I can see where she wouldn't want her last remaining link to family—even if it is a family she previously wanted nothing to do with—being signed away to a virtual stranger."

"But that's just it," Jake said, leaning forward in

his chair. "I'm not the stranger here—at least not to Bonnie."

Mrs. Starling lowered her gaze, making a slight clucking sound before once again glancing his way. "I'm so sorry about all of this. I've seen you and the infant together. The way the child seems so at peace when she rests her little cheek on your shoulder. Precious. Just precious. Believe me," she said, gesturing to all of her pictures. "No one likes happy endings more than me. These photos, they aren't just snapshots, they're my life. My successes. Tangible proof that I've turned healing broken hearts into my life's work." Again lowering her gaze, she added, "Unfortunately, for all of these smiling faces, I've seen an awful lot of tears."

On the edge of his seat, proverbial hat in his hands, Jake swallowed hard.

Yeah, well, if I have anything to say about it, tears you'll never see are mine or my baby's.

To anyone else, it might sound selfish, but what this woman didn't realize was that it wasn't just Bonnie's future at stake, but his.

Growing up, he'd had an idyllic childhood. His parents were the best—especially his dad. Which was probably one of the reasons Jake had always wanted to be a dad. To do the Little League and birthday party routine. To help with homework and to tuck freshly scrubbed rug rats into bed.

After marrying Candy, his high school sweetheart, Jake had thought all of those dreams were finally within reach. But that was before she'd become obsessed with her business and started spouting non-sense about never wanting to be a mom.

He thought he'd die from the pain when, after five years of marriage, Candy had filed for divorce. But ten years after signing the papers, here he was, still going strong without her—or any woman. Here he was, holding steadfast to his vow to never again fall victim to love, and to his conviction that if it took a wife to have children, then he'd just have to suffer through life without them.

When Cal and Jenny died, fate had given Jake his dream after all. Finally, finally, he was a dad, and no matter what it took, there was no way in hell he was giving up his precious baby girl.

"Look," he said, softening his voice. "I *can* do this. The diaper changing, bottle washing, shopping for prom dresses—none of it's a problem. Besides which, I'm all Bonnie's got. Her parents weren't just friends, but family."

"In a strictly nonrelated way. You must understand, Mr. Peterson, I can't hand out babies to anyone who asks. There are procedures to follow, all of which center around not just the current well-being of this infant, but her future, as well. Please don't think for a minute that I don't believe you'd make an excellent father. All I'm saying is that sometimes judges…well, they tend to side with the law, which all too often sees these matters as being neatly tied with a bow when the man or woman appointed custody also happen to be a blood relative."

"But that's not right—or fair. In Elizabeth Mannford's case, her being a member of Bonnie's family is nothing more than semantics.''

Lips pursed, Mrs. Starling said, ''I'm afraid you're right. Now, if you were married, I could maybe—''

''What?''

She scrunched her nose. ''Excuse me?''

''That last part,'' he said, making a hurry-up gesture. ''Come again on that last part.''

''I was only pointing out that if you had a wife, then— Oh, my. A *wife*. That's it. Why didn't I think of that?'' Her gray eyes sparkled in direct proportion to the lifting in his heart. ''Mr. Peterson? Where are you going?''

Leaving the office, Jake let out a whoop. ''Where do you think I'm going? To my country club. Surely there's a blonde lounging around the pool who'll temporarily marry me.''

''Not so fast!'' Mrs. Starling shouted.

Stopping dead in his tracks, Jake groaned. ''Now what?''

''Come back here. I see where you're headed with this and while I must admit to being wholeheartedly in favor of your plan, you can't marry a stranger. Any family judge worth his or her salt will see right through that old trick. No, what you need is an honest-to-goodness relationship. A loving relationship in which you share not just a future with a woman, but a past.'' She paused, flashing him a hopeful smile. ''You've got to have known this woman for a lifetime. Long enough to trust with every fiber of your being that she'd make a loving mother and wife. Long enough to know she'll stand by you through a long, and quite possibly nasty, legal battle.''

Popping another butterscotch into her mouth, she said, ''There now. Finding a wonderful woman like that doesn't sound too terribly difficult, does it?''

Jake's stomach fell the three flights of stairs he'd climbed to get to Mrs. Starling's office.

Was the woman nuts?

Because from where he was sitting, he could only think of one woman in his life who'd ever even remotely fit such a lofty bill. Candy. In his mind's eye, he clearly recalled her pretty smile and eyes so deliciously brown, that just meeting her gaze was akin to sinking in a vat of sinfully rich melted chocolate.

Unfortunately, the last time he'd been looking into those eyes, his ex-wife hadn't been smiling. She'd been crying. And the sight of those tears hadn't just ripped his heart in two, but made him adhere to a strict vow to never, ever get married again.

So now, here he was being told the only possible way he could keep baby Bonnie was to not only marry again, but to marry the one woman on the planet who'd torn his life apart?

In a perfect world, he'd oh-so-politely tell Mrs. Starling right where she could put her ludicrous suggestion. Problem was, his world was nowhere close to perfect, and if he didn't go along with her suggestion, he wouldn't even have a world—that was how strong his bond to Bonnie had become.

Steeling his jaw, Jake reached an inevitable conclusion. As unpalatable—hell, as downright unthinkable—as it sounded, if he was to have even a prayer of keeping Bonnie, he'd have to once again marry Candy. Fast!

Chapter One

Three days later...

In super-stealth mode, Jake Peterson stepped onto the brick step of the Candy Kisses Confectioner's Shop and Ice Cream Parlor. But just as he was about to launch the most important merger meeting of his life, his cell phone rang.

Cursing himself for not leaving the stupid thing in his rental car, he answered, "Yeah?"

"Did you do it?"

"Hell, no, I didn't do it." He ducked out of the unseasonably hot Missouri May sun and into the shade of a bush trimmed into the shape of a— Was that a giant cat? On the branches of the cat's belly, a flock of starlings bickered like toddlers vying for the teacher's last animal cracker. Covering his left ear, Jake said, "I thought I told you to wait for me to call you."

"I know, but I've got a baby question."

"What?"

"Bonnie's poop's lookin' a little *off*."

"What do you mean?"

"I don't know, man, it's kind of purple. Something about it just isn't right. And it smells a little like cat-fish bait."

Jake sighed before asking Rick, his best friend from high school and now the manager of the original Galaxy Sports Store, located a few doors down from where he now stood, "What did you guys feed her? I've only been gone fifteen minutes."

"Creamed chicken and some leftover noodle stuff—oh, and Dietz let her have a grape Popsicle. Man, you should've seen that little gal sucking away. Oh—and right after you left, she gummed a cherry Pop-Tart."

"And did that make her poop red?"

"Come to think of it…"

Jake brushed his left hand over his face. Having grown up and later worked with most of the guys now manning the store, he'd thought they were all capable of watching Bonnie for a few hours. But maybe he'd been wrong. Come to think of it, maybe he was wrong to have even thought about setting foot back in this town. "Where's Warren?" he asked.

"He got a call from his kid's school. Millicent got knocked in the front tooth during gym class and he had to take her to the dentist."

Great. So the only guy in the store with practical parenting skills was gone. "Look, Rick, baby poop is literally a fluid situation. Changes all the time. Don't worry about it unless—well, hell, just don't worry. And don't call me for at least the next thirty minutes. I'm going in."

"LET'S SEE…I'll take two Coco Locos, a Dino Bar, and a chocolate-covered strawberry."

"Mmm, I like your style." Without looking up, Candy Jacobs-Peterson opened the glass storage case and gave the confections housed inside an appreciative whiff. Even after all her years in the candy business, she still loved the rich smell of her creations.

She reached for a piece of tissue, then snatched a couple of her most celebrated masterpieces. The milk chocolate, almond and toasted coconut Coco Loco blend outsold her other candies three to one. At Monday's closing, she'd have to remind Candy Kisses' new owners to make extra for the weekend rush.

Hard to believe that a week from today, the business that had become her family would be sold. For all practical purposes, she'd never had a mother. After her dad had died when she was eleven, she'd been raised by her grandfather right here in this store. Her brief marriage to Jake had started out as a blessing, but ultimately, as she'd feared it would, fallen victim to her curse.

After her divorce, Candy had returned to the store and her grandfather, believing that hard work would be the cure for whatever ailed her. For a while, it had been enough. But when he died and, over the year since he'd been gone, despite receiving comfort from many dear friends, the loneliness had consumed her.

She'd felt lost. Adrift.

And now…

Now, she needed more. Of what, she had no clue.

Yes, you do.

Candy ignored her conscience's nudge toward unthinkable directions. Truly, something was missing from her life. But whatever that elusive something was, she'd had no luck finding it here in Lonesome, the only town where she'd ever lived. Which was why, first thing next Monday morning, she planned to sign the sale papers for Candy Kisses, close up her house, then leave Lonesome for however long it would take to find peace.

She swallowed a fresh batch of jitters to hand the customer his distinctive pink box that had her kindergarten picture right on the front, lips puckered for a kiss. "Can I get you anything el—"

The box, along with its contents, tumbled to the floor, hitting glowing hardwood with a soft thwack. Candy fluttered her hands to her mouth. "Oh, my gosh...Jake."

He matched her shock with a wry smile. "That happy to see me, huh?"

"It's not that—well, it's just that I..." *Pull yourself together,* she admonished. So what if it's been ten years? So what if he's grown taller, darker and infinitely more handsome? Just treat him like any other customer.

Easily enough said, but how many other customers broke your heart?

"In town for the reunion?" she asked, trying to play it cool while kneeling to clean up the mess.

"Yep. I thought I wasn't going to make it, but at the last minute..." She stood in time to see him shrug. "You know how plans change."

"Yes, well..." No one knew that better than her.

"It's good that you could make it after all. I know the guys down at the store must be glad to see you."

What about you, Candy? Are you glad to see me? Jake reminded himself to breathe.

His ex had always been a knockout, but now…

He swallowed hard, forcing himself to look past her whiskey-brown eyes, honeyed complexion and too-damned-sexy, sable-toned hair. In the millisecond it took to blink, he pictured her lounging in bed, wearing that ivory-silk negligee she'd bought *him* for their first wedding anniversary. Fine lace played hide-and-seek with her breasts while from behind her half curtain of sleek, dark waves, she grinned, beckoning him closer, inviting him to unwrap his gift.

Jake released a sharp breath.

Focus, man. Remember, you're in town to find a temporary mom for Bonnie—not a playmate for you.

Besides, Jake reminded himself, being burned once by Candy's particularly painful brand of rejection had been more than enough to scar his lifetime.

"So," he said with a light clap, rubbing his palms together. "The guys told me you're about to start a new project."

"I suppose that's one way of putting it," she said, straightening the already-perfectly-aligned jars of her signature ice-cream toppings.

"So? What're you doing? Finally launching a new store? Some hot new candy you're taking nationwide?"

Shifting two jars to a higher shelf, she stood on her tiptoes, raising her arms high enough for her breasts to strain the buttons of her white silk blouse. Finished, she said, "You were the only one around here with global dreams, Jake. Mine have always been simple." A ghostly smile playing about her lips, she shook her head. "I can't believe the guys didn't tell you."

Tell me what? That you're hotter than ever?

He gulped. "How come I'm feeling like I'm the only one in town who doesn't know?"

"In case you've forgotten, Jake, we're kind of divorced."

"Touché."

Averting her gaze, she said, "Wow. I can't get over the fact that you're really here. The last person I expected to see today was you." When she again looked his way, she'd captured long strands of her hair between her fingers, intently twirling it as if the action would fix whatever was causing the sadness in her eyes.

The last time Jake had seen her twirl her hair was the day she'd signed their divorce papers.

"Candy," he said, stepping closer to the counter. "Is something wrong? I mean, besides seeing me?" He flashed her a weak grin, which she answered with one of her own.

"No. It's just that this is a pretty strange day."

"How so? It's just another Monday, isn't it?"

Her nod was followed by a tiny hiccup, which was in turn followed by a gasping sob. "Oh, Jake, I know I'm making the right decision, but…"

In a heartbeat he stormed behind the counter and pulled her close. "Shh…" he said, stroking her hair while at the same time denying a strange sense of déjà vu. "Whatever's going on with you, Candy, I'm sure everything's going to be okay."

As if only just now realizing that he held her in his arms, she stepped back, gazing up at him with a teary-eyed wonder that quickly turned to distrust. "Look at me," she said, wiping her cheeks with the backs of her hands. She took another step back and straightened her hair. "Here I am, on the threshold of the biggest adventure of my life, and acting as if it's some kind of jail sentence."

Jake scratched his head. "Mind explaining all that for those of us who showed up late to the party?"

"Oops," she said with a brave smile. "I forgot that you don't know. Today is my last Monday standing behind this counter." She washed her fingers over the timeworn white marble. "A week from today I'm selling Candy Kisses and leaving Lonesome."

"Temporarily, right?"

"No. That's the most exciting part. First, I'm crossing the Andes—on a llama! It's one of those adventure/eco trips. And then there's my Amazon cruise, and from there, the Galapagos, and—"

"But wh-what about your grandfather?" Dear Lord, what was she thinking? Candy Kisses had been in her family for more than fifty years. Candy Kisses *was* her family. She couldn't just sell it.

"You didn't know that, either? Grandpa died last spring."

Jake washed his face with his hands, released a deep-throated groan. "Jeez, I'm so sorry... But that makes your wanting to sell all the more baffling. Woman, have you lost your mind?"

"Excuse me?"

"You're selling the only thing in your life you've ever really loved in exchange for riding some hairy beast through the Andes? What is this? Some kind of harebrained attempt to *find* yourself?"

"Yes—I mean, no. And what if it is? What gives you the right to question anything I do? And you don't have to make it sound as if my trip is some whacked-out, New Age spiritual thing. It's just a vacation. A chance to see new things. Meet new people." *A chance to figure out what I want to do with the rest of my life.*

Candy brushed past Jake, ignoring the icy-hot tingles where the cramped space forced their arms and hips to touch.

"Where are you going?"

Without looking back, she answered, "Home. I have a lot of packing to do." From out of the cabinet at the end of the counter, she snatched her purse.

"You're just going to leave the store? I thought you stayed open late every night of the week?"

"Only Thursday through Sunday."

"Yeah, but what about today's customers?"

"They'll come back tomorrow."

"What kind of business plan is that? You've got to seize the market. Be ready to close the deal on even the smallest sale."

Heading for the front entrance, she said, "At the moment, Jake, the only thing I'm closing is the door. Last warning or you'll be spending the night."

In one of those grandiose moves only her ex would even think about pulling off, he braced his hands on the short counter and swung his legs over. Sure enough, he beat her to the door and now stood, arms crossed, blocking it.

"You haven't grown an emotional inch, have you?"

"Oh, like you have? Hiding from whatever's eating you by cutting it out of your life?"

"I'm not hiding. I'm going home to pack."

"Packing for your trip to run off and hide."

Tears welled at the backs of Candy's eyes and she stubbornly forced them away. It had taken years to stop crying herself to sleep over this man. No way would she give him the satisfaction of crying over him now. Had he forgotten what he put her through? Had he forgotten what kind of pain she'd put aside just in trusting him enough to marry him?

He'd known what kind of rotten family she'd come from. He'd known, and yet he hadn't cared. For if he had cared, he wouldn't have pressured her for so much more than she would have ever been able to give.

"If we're talking about running, Jake," she said, taking a deep, calming breath, "I'm not the one who left the only home he's ever known to whoop it up on Florida's beaches."

"We're not talking about me, Candy, we're talking about you, still avoiding your problems."

"What problems?" she asked a little too shrilly. "Until you, the Official Playboy of the Entire Eastern Seaboard, showed up, life was looking good."

"There you go, blaming your troubles on me."

"Argh, I guess some things never change. Add the

two of us mixing like oil and water to that list. I thought your showing up out of the blue for the reunion was some kind of sign. You know, that you had finally put the past behind you and we could at least act civilized toward each other. But I guess I was wrong.''

Fumbling through her purse for her keys, she was again fighting back tears, telling herself that it was saying farewell to her store that had her in such a dither. "You *never* understood me." *Understood what I gave up for you.* "And who are you to lecture me about my faults, when there you are, day after day, throwing it all away.''

"Throwing what away?"

Your big chance, Jake. Your chance to be the one thing you could never be with me. The one thing I know you wanted above anything else—especially me. The chance to become a father. Keys in hand, Candy pressed her lips tight.

"Answer me." Gripping her shoulders, he gave her a light squeeze. "What was that last comment supposed to mean?"

"Nothing. I don't know."

"Bull!" Jake released her along with a wall of pent-up air. His back to her, he raked his fingers through his hair. This whole scene was out of control. He'd intended this to be a clean-cut mission. In, propose, out. One, two, three. So where had he gone wrong?

Funny how that was the same question he'd faced the last time they'd fought.

If he knew what was good for him, he'd leave right

now and take his chances with hiring a woman to play
the role of his wife. Maybe he could even answer one
of those mysterious ads in the backs of magazines that
promised to create false IDs and personal histories in
thirty days or less.

Yeah right, and maybe donkeys fly south for the
winter.

*Face it, bud, the only shot you've got at keeping
Bonnie is standing right in front of you, staring you
down as though she'd just as soon spit on you than
look at you.*

"Jake," she said in an uncharacteristically small
voice. "Why are you *really* here? And don't give me
that line about being in town for the reunion, because
Page Watson told me six weeks ago that you wrote
'Return to Sender' on the outside of your invitation."

Six weeks ago, Cal and Jenny had still been alive.

And Candy was right. Ordinarily, Jake wouldn't
have shown up at their class reunion for all the beer
in St. Louis. Sure, he would've loved hanging out
with the guys, but given the very good chance that
he'd also run into Candy…thank you very much, but
he'd have more fun in bankruptcy court.

That being the case, again, why not walk away?
Hop the next flight for Palm Breeze and never look
back?

Bonnie, that's why.

Flashes of cute chubby cheeks, heart-melting tooth-
less grins, silky-soft tufts of hair and the scent of
freshly washed and lotioned baby tummy not only
steeled his resolve, but took the decision out of his
hands and put it squarely in the hands of fate.

Hardening his jaw, he said, "You're right. The re-union was an excuse. I'm really here to talk to you."

"About what?"

"Marriage. Or to be more specific...*our* marriage. And the question of whether or not you'd be ame-nable to starting it back up?"

Jake couldn't tell whether Candy had parted her ripe lips to speak or was caught in a gasp. Either way, he wasn't sure he wanted to know. He'd meant to thaw her a little before popping the mother of all questions, but dammit, given his time crunch—not to mention her travel plans—there wasn't a whole helluva lot else he could do.

"I-I...I'm sorry," she said, her voice breathy, as if his suggestion had knocked the wind from her lungs. "I don't know what to say."

"Say you'll have dinner with me tonight and in-stead of fighting, we'll talk—even better, say you'll cook dinner for me."

"B-but—"

"Great," he said with a wide grin. "I'll be at your place at seven."

Chapter Two

"What's with the corn dogs?" Candy's best friend and neighbor, Kelly Foster, asked at six forty-five that night.

"You think I should've made Jake a standing rib roast?"

From her perch on one of the tall stools lining the burgundy-tiled counter, Kelly made a face. "At least spaghetti and a salad would have been nice. I mean, come on, corn dogs? The guy asked you to marry him again, not scrub his toilets."

"True," Candy said, pulling open the oven door and sliding in the tray of dogs. "And, hey, at least this time around he's loaded. He can afford a dozen housekeepers to do all the dirty work. Think they clean up broken hearts?"

For a brief second, she squeezed her eyes shut while forcing back tears. Sarcasm wasn't like her, which proved that the sooner Jake returned to Florida, the better off her mood—not to mention, life—would be. "Sorry to be so testy," Candy said. "It's just that where Jake Peterson is concerned, one marriage was way more than enough."

Kelly rolled her eyes. "From your first bizarre date spent picnicking on the Lonesome High football field, you two were made for each other. Everyone knows it. Why do you think Jake never married again?"

"How should I know? We haven't exactly stayed close. And for your information, our first date wasn't bizarre, it was romantic." Candy threw extra force into whacking a freezer-burned bag of French fries against the butcher-block cutting board.

"Eww," Kelly said. "How old are those?"

"Judging by the ice pack's density, I'd make a conservative guess that I bought them around the time I broke up with Chad. Remember that grease phase I went through?" Candy shuddered. "My skin breaks out just thinking about it. At least one good thing is coming out of this dinner."

"What's that?"

"I'm cleaning out the freezer."

Grinning, Kelly shook her pretty blond head. "You're hopeless. Back to the subject of Jake, what do you think he's up to?"

"You mean, besides no good? *Ba-bum ching.*" While tapping the high hat on her imaginary drums, Candy flashed her friend a smile.

"You're not fooling me, you know."

Reaching into the fridge for mustard and ketchup, Candy said, "I wasn't trying to."

"You're scared to death, aren't you?"

"About what? This is just dinner. I do it every night of the week, every week of the year—except during our annual cruise, and then I do it two times a night. *Ba-bum ching.*'' Using the ketchup bottle as a microphone, she said in a deep Elvis voice, ''Thank you, thank you very much. You can catch my act nightly at the Lonesome Lounge.''

''This is bad. Very bad.'' Leaning her right elbow on the counter, Kelly cupped her chin in her hand. Tapping her cheek with her index finger, she said, ''I haven't seen you this un-funny since the night you heard Jake was leaving for Florida.''

''What are you talking about?'' Candy said, filling two glasses with iced tea. ''We celebrated that night. Remember? I sprung for all of us girls to eat the Holiday Motel's seafood buffet. It was a lot of fun.''

''Of course, how could I forget a thrill-a-minute evening of culinary delights like crab-flavored chicken wings—not to mention the fact that you must've told enough cornball jokes to keep Laffy Taffy in business for the next hundred years. Come on,'' Kelly said with a sigh. ''It's me you're talking to. You can tell me how you really feel.''

''How many times do I have to say this,'' Candy said, putting the mustard and ketchup in the dishwasher. ''I feel fine. I'm not the least bit upset about Jake being back in town.'' One by one, she started to unload mugs from the top rack and slide them onto the brass hooks beneath the cabinets.

''Is it because you're on such an emotional high that you've decided to unload the dishes before even washing them?''

Candy gazed at the assorted dribbles of coffee, tea, and cocoa pooling on the counter. ''Crap.''

"What was that? Miss Sunshine isn't actually a tad on edge is she?"

"No," Candy all but growled.

"Good, then when you finish *reloading* all those dirty mugs, you might want to *unload* the ketchup and mustard."

A squeal of pure panic escaped Candy's lips. "Oh, God. I *am* a wreck, aren't I? Kelly, you've got to stay through dinner. What am I going to do? Say? I can't be alone with him. You know what just looking at Jake does to me. I mean, I despise him, but that doesn't mean I don't still think he's the hottest guy on the planet. I mean, you should've seen him at the store today, his hair all mussed and that disgustingly handsome chiseled jawline of his all freshly shaven and tanned. And his bod—don't even get me started on what ten years have done for the man's physique." When Candy's shoulders slumped, her best friend hopped off her stool to enfold her in a hug.

"Trust me," Kelly said, "you're going to be fine. You two were high school sweethearts. You've known each other forever. Maybe, just maybe," she said, brushing away one of Candy's tears, "he misses you, and that proposal was more real than you think."

"Fat chance," Candy said through one last sniffle. "Even if I wanted to get back together with him— which I don't—you weren't here the morning he came home to pick up the last of his stuff. I handed him the shoe box he kept my love letters in, but he told me to keep it, Kel. He told me he didn't want a single thing in his new life to remind him of me. After that, he walked out. He didn't even say goodbye."

"Thanks," Kelly said, using a paper towel to blot at her own tears. "Now you've got me all choked up, too—and I'm supposed to be the strong one." She pulled Candy into a fierce hug.

"*Please* stay for dinner," Candy whined. "I'll make you a steak—oh, and those twice-baked potatoes you love." A sharp metallic noise called her gaze to the window. "Oh, no, was that a car door?"

"See ya," Kelly said, pulling back with a wave of her paper hanky.

"What about your steak? You love my steaks."

Kelly blew her a kiss on her way out the back door. "I also love you, which is why I think it'd be best for you to handle this one on your own. Besides which, not only do I have a watercolor class tonight, but I happen to know for a fact you have nothing in that fridge of yours besides moldy cheese and three-year-old pickles. 'Bye."

"Deserter," Candy mumbled, watching her only link to sanity fairly skip across the backyard.

The doorbell rang.

The screen door creaked open. "Candy? You in there?"

She crossed through the living room on her way to the front door.

"Hi," was all she could think to say when, just like when she'd been a new bride watching her groom saunter into the house, Jake's lopsided grin tumbled her heart.

"Something smells good," he said. "What's for dinner?"

"Corn dogs."

"Yum. My favorite."

Had he always been so tall? The room never used to feel cramped when he was in it. And why was she suddenly wishing she'd taken Kelly's advice and at least made a quick batch of spaghetti? "Sorry I didn't fix a more substantial meal. I'm basically running low on everything."

"Who's complaining?" he said, gazing around the comfortable room with what she hoped was appreciation.

They'd bought the once-nearly-condemned Queen Anne not long after their wedding because the payments had been cheaper than rent. The rambling home sat atop a forested hill overlooking Lonesome Lake. Over the years she'd restored the place to its former glory, and though she couldn't fathom why, it meant a lot to her that Jake liked what she'd done.

Licking her lips, she said, "A lot's changed around here since you left."

"I'll say." He let loose with a low whistle. "It actually looks cozy instead of like the poorest frat house on campus. What happened to the cement-block bookshelves and Goldilocks—that old gold sofa we had to prop up with leftover bathroom tiles?"

"They died. They're now at the city dump, resting in peace beside a lovely retired couple. You might know them. The Kenmores? Adorable pair of washer and dryers. Used to live over on Pecan Lane in a yellow ranch."

Jake's chuckle caught Candy off guard, filling her with velvety images of the past. Breakfasts and dinners shared upon a wobbly sawhorse table. Saturday night candlelit bubble baths, exchanging off-color jokes as to why the hot water pipes groaned. For a second, Candy's world felt right again, the way it used to. Back in the days when if only she could make Jake laugh, everything would be okay.

A pang shot through her at the realization of just how *not* okay those old days had turned out to be.

Since the last thing she wanted Jake knowing was how topsy-turvy his presence made her feel, she played tour guide. "On the left, you'll see my sort-of-new sofa. Note the soft floral chintz. Always a big hit during the occasional bridal shower I get wheedled into hosting. And to the right, we have a real, live bookshelf/entertainment unit—I'm still working on the entertainment part."

"Nice," Jake said with a slow nod. "But how do you see what's on TV? It's awfully small. I didn't even know they made that size for home use."

"Well, now you do. Besides, it suits me just fine since now that the house is done, my nights are usually spent reading or doing the shop's books."

"That's all well and good, Candy, but if you want a big screen TV, all you have to do is—"

"Thank you, but I don't want your money, Jake."

"It's *our* money."

"You formed the current-day Galaxy Sports *after* our divorce."

"Yeah, but in the divorce papers, it states quite clearly that you're a half owner."

"But I don't want to be."

"Tough. You are."

"Argh!" she said, ducking her gaze from his intense dark one. "Ten years certainly hasn't put a dent in your pride."

They stood only three feet apart but, in that instant, they might as well have been on separate planets. What was it about him that after all this time still turned her legs to taffy? Part of her wanted nothing more than to drop the pretense of not-so-polite chit-chat and get to the reasons for his sudden—not to mention ludicrous—proposal. But another part of her, the part fighting a bizarre desire to drag the man back into her life, to lock him up and throw away the key, felt that the more casual they kept this meeting, the better.

"I know this'll sound strange," he said, "but once I tell you why I'm here, you'll see just how little pride I have left."

"I'm all ears." She mimed bunny ears at the sides of her head, wiggling her fingers in a feeble attempt to disguise a nervous giggle.

"Okay, well…" He sniffed, looked toward the kitchen. "Is that smoke? Jeez, Candy, from the looks of it, your whole damned kitchen's on fire!"

A FEW MINUTES LATER Jake had extinguished supper, but a thick, not to mention, smelly, gray cloud still clung to the ceiling. On the scary meter, the oven flame-up had been nothing compared to the white-hot terror stuck in his throat at the mere possibility of Candy being in danger. Now that he knew she'd be okay, he felt even worse.

Because really, he had no business worrying about her.

For a minute there, he'd felt as though they were married again, as though she was still his responsibility.

"Well, that oughtta do it," he said, setting the extinguisher on the counter before adding, in what he hoped was a carefree tone, "Good thing I carry that model in all of my stores. If I hadn't been familiar with how it works, your kitchen might be toast."

"Yeah," Candy said from beside the sink. Already having opened the windows and turned on the fan, she now wielded the faucet's spray attachment—just in case. "Guess I'd better start keeping a closer eye on those rascally corn dogs, huh?"

"Might be a good idea—especially when you set the oven on broil."

"Oops. I thought I'd set it on three-fifty. Guess before you got here I was sort of wound up."

A charming blush pinkened her cheeks, but it did little to quench his frustration with her for being so careless. Didn't she know how much she meant to him?

Whoa, buddy. Shouldn't that be how much she *used* to mean? Because now, a reunion with Candy only meant one thing: keeping Bonnie.

Leaning against the counter, he turned serious. "I'm afraid you're going to need a new oven."

"You think?"

He nodded and crossed to where she stood. Hands on her shoulders, in his best manly fireman voice, he said, "It's okay, ma'am. Fire's out. You can safely put down the hose." Easily enough said, but the jolt zinging through his arms from just touching her made him think he was the one in danger from fire. The flames leaping from her!

He must not have been the only one affected by their touch. Candy not only popped the spray nozzle back into its hole, she scooted a good two feet down the counter.

In all the excitement, she'd earned a black smudge of courage across her left cheek. Years of watching out for her leaned him forward, where, with the pad of his thumb, he brushed away the soot.

"What're you—" She tensed until she realized what he was doing.

"Sorry, you had some—"

"It's okay." Her dusky gaze darted to the floor, then back to him. "Thanks. For the cleanup job and for saving our—I mean, *my* house."

"No problem." Had he only imagined it, or was the Ice Queen starting to thaw? "Glad I was here to help."

"Yeah. Me, too." Candy gave herself a mental thwack on the head. *Yeah. Me, too?* What was wrong with her? For a second there, she'd actually enjoyed his company.

Time for a reality check. And the lonely reality was that no matter how right Jake's being back in their kitchen might feel, his presence was only temporary.

Which was good.

Because, really, she was far better off without him.

How could she have forgotten how relieved she'd been when he'd left? How great it had felt knowing she'd never hear him ask those tired old questions again?

"When do you want to start our family?" he'd asked morning, noon and night. "You're gorgeous. Only in my dreams can I imagine how adorable our kids are going to be." Nuzzling her neck, he'd follow up with, "Any idea how soon we can expect to be expecting?" And toward the end of their marriage, "Come on, Candy Cane. I'm just asking for a couple of kids. How bad could they be?"

Candy swallowed hard, watching through watery eyes as the only man she'd ever loved sauntered to the fridge.

Head inside, giving her an entirely too attractive view of his tight, jeans-clad derriere, he said, "I'm hungry, woman. What's to eat around here besides—" he pulled out a jar, squinting at the label "—mini-gherkins?"

Hurriedly wiping at a stray tear, she said, "Ketchup or mustard. Take your pick."

"You need to go to the store. This is no way to live."

"Ordinarily, I'd say you're right, but in case you forgot, I'm leaving for Peru in six days, so there's not much need for stocking up."

He closed the fridge, eyed the now soggy bag of fries. "Wanna order a pizza?"

"Nah, let's save money and play food scavenger hunt."

"Why? There's no need to save money."

"For you, maybe."

"Candy," Jake said, softening his tone. "Half of everything Galaxy Sports has ever made is sitting in an account with your name on it. Why won't you use it?''

''Simple, because I don't want *your* money.''

''It's *our* money. Dad gave that business to me *and* you on our first anniversary. Remember? The divorce papers say all profits are to be split fifty/fifty.''

''For the last time, Jake, please listen. Thank you for the offer. It's sweet—beyond sweet. But really, I don't want or need it. Give the money to charity. Send a few kids to college.'' She turned her back on him, knotting her arms across her chest.

''More than a few kids. We're talking millions of dollars, Candy.''

''Oh, so is that the going rate for a woman's heart?''

''What's that supposed to mean?''

She spun around to face him. ''What do you think it means? Sure, we fought a lot about how you wanted kids, but beyond that, Galaxy Sports also contributed to our marriage falling apart. Because you started caring more about proving to your dad how good you were at selling everything from footballs to fishing poles than you ever cared about being my husband.''

''Wrong. If memory serves me correctly, you spent an awful lot of time at Candy Kisses, too. What was I supposed to do, turn caveman and drag you home? The more I thought about it, the more I realized maybe you'd never wanted to be my wife.''

''That's not true,'' she said, her voice a raspy whisper. She swallowed hard, fighting still more tears clinging to the corners of her eyes. ''You know why I asked for a divorce. It was about kids, Jake. Your obsessive need for them. I told you I couldn't have them, but you wouldn't listen. You knew I could never be a mom. You knew it, yet you kept bringing up the subject—despite the fact that you also knew how much it hurt me to let you go.''

"*Let* me go?" He laughed. "More like booted me out the door."

"Argh, this is just like you, you stubborn— Never mind. Evidently my reasons don't matter any more now than they did ten years ago."

"What reasons? That's just it. You never gave me any. I could live without having kids, what I couldn't live without was love, Candy. And let's face it, when that last year went by with us living like strangers, what was I supposed to think? And when you filed for divorce… Well, I know I can be thick-headed, but it wouldn't have taken a jackhammer to pound the fact into me that at that point you pretty much didn't give a damn about me or our marriage."

"That's where you're wrong." She aimed her index finger in the direction of his chest, ignoring the release of ten years' worth of hot tears. "I—I would have done anything for you. That's how much I *used* to love you, Jake. I loved you so much that I set you free. I couldn't give you kids, so I set you free to have them with another woman. That's how much I loved you—not Candy Kisses—*you*."

"Jeez." He slashed his fingers through his hair and haltingly approached her before going for broke and crushing her in a hug. "Oh, man, Candy. What a mess we made of things, huh?"

She nodded against his warm, oh-so-solid chest.

Being back in his arms felt so good, so right, as if she'd finally come home. Too bad that home was just a dream. The fairy tale the two of them once shared could never be recreated.

Those once-idyllic days had been back when they were lovesick teens. Married at eighteen, only a month after their high school graduation, their marriage lasted a whole five years. At first, it'd been idyllic. With both of them working long hours in their respective family businesses, they hadn't given a thought to the future aside from what time they'd next make love. For nearly twelve months, that had been enough, but then Jake had wanted more.

The total package—meaning kids.

He knew what kind of mother she'd had. The whole town knew the sad cliché of poor little Candy Jacobs's mother running off—never to be seen again—with a traveling carpet company rep she'd met at the interior design shop where she worked.

Even before that, though, Valerie Jacobs could hardly have been nominated for mother of the year. She didn't bake cookies, read bedtime stories or attend school plays. She never cooed over scribbled drawings or A-plus spelling tests, and she certainly never braided her daughter's hair or shopped hand in hand for the perfect Easter dress. Not that any of that would have even mattered to Candy had she provided the one thing every child craved above all else—love.

No, the worst thing about Valerie Jacobs was that she'd been devoid of feelings for anyone but herself—oh, and of course, for her lovers.

Candy's dad had tried making up for her mother's

shortcomings with occasional pats on the head and hugs, but he was always busy at work, trying to keep her mother in the finery that only occasionally made her smile.

Years after the fact, Candy had learned that the man her mom had finally run off with hadn't even been her first affair.

When her father died of a heart attack three days after Valerie's abandonment, no one had been surprised. They'd just amended the gossip to include the fact that ''that Jacobs woman'' had quite literally broken her husband's heart.

When Candy's grandfather had taken her in, life had been a little sweeter. But the little girl who eventually grew up never forgot the kind of emptiness that lurked inside. After all, half of her blood was Valerie's, which meant she was destined by DNA to be just as wretched a wife and mom. The only question was when the time bomb ticking inside her would finally go off.

Jake had known all about Candy's mother. What he hadn't known—because she'd never told him— was that Candy had no intention of repeating her mother's mistakes. When Jake began pressuring her to have kids, Candy realized she had already made one disastrous error in ever daring to dream she'd make a good wife. Hurting herself and Jake had been one thing. But her most sacred vow, no matter what, she wouldn't break. And that was to never, *ever* become a mother herself. No child deserved the lonely life she'd once led.

Jake softly stroked her hair, so softly that had

Candy been a cat, she would have flopped onto her back and purred. Problem was, she wasn't a cat. She was a flesh-and-blood woman who needed to get on with life.

Life without Jake.

Jake stiffened when Candy pulled away.

After sniffling, she said, "I'm sorry. I didn't mean to go all emotional on you. What I meant to say is that if you'd like a pizza, since I'm tonight's hostess, I'll buy."

"Sure," he said, tucking his hands into his jean's pockets, warming them because after releasing her, bone-chilling loneliness licked the tips of his fingers. "That sounds good—only I'm paying."

"Okay," she said with a wooden nod. "I'll go call."

Alone in the comfortable kitchen with its yellow-gingham curtains, hanging copper pots and glowing oak cabinets, Jake felt lost. Out of his comfort zone. His world was modern and sleek. Filled with man stuff. Chrome and leather and women who didn't even know a kitchen came with their mansions. He'd come here to ask Candy a simple question. What had gone wrong?

In spite of Candy's confession that, at least in her mind, her reasons for divorcing him had been entirely altruistic, that didn't mean their main dispute had changed.

He still wanted kids, she didn't. Period. Not just end of story, end of *their* story.

If he were smart, he'd walk away.

But he wasn't smart, he was in love—not with

Candy—but Bonnie. And if that made him a fool for love, then so be it.

Gazing around the kitchen, taking in the handmade rag rug hugging the brick floor, the candid photos gracing buttercream-yellow walls, the beams of warm twilight shafting through the paned bay window to kiss the ladder-backed chairs at a round oak table, he realized with a lonely ache that this was the kind of home he'd grown up in.

This was the kind of home he wanted for Bonnie.

Oh, sure, he could have Palm Breeze's hottest designer turn his house into a carbon copy of Candy's, but what he couldn't pay someone to reproduce was the everyday simplicity. The deep-down sweetness.

The scent of painstakingly rubbed lemon oil that did battle with burnt corn dogs and won. The happy gurgle of a fish tank bubbling in the far corner. And from outside the screened windows, faint stirrings of leaves in the trees. Waves lapping at the lakeshore. Kids playing Freeze Tag somewhere down the street.

After all that Jake had achieved, the fortune he'd amassed, this kitchen was the one thing that, in as long as he could remember, felt familiar. Like home. It irked him that just being back in this room, no matter how much in appearances it'd changed, inside, he felt the same way he had walking out for the last time. Like an empty, aimless shell of a man.

Dammit, but he resented Candy for going on with her life and this house without him.

This had been *his* house as much as hers. His dream as much as hers. And now, seeing how capably she'd managed without him, he felt like an intruder.

A failure. And that scared him, for the only thing he'd ever in his whole life failed at was his relationship with her.

How ironic was it that his future with Bonnie depended on his past with his ex-wife?

Just like his dad, he'd always planned on returning home after a long day's work not to an empty house, but to a home bursting with laughter and life. Kids, dogs, cats, hamsters— Once upon a time Jake had wanted it all, with Candy beside him, hugging him, kissing him, making love to him late into the night until they had to stop because one of their kids was banging on the bedroom door.

"Mommy? Daddy? Can I come in? I had a bad dream."

Candy would giggle, pulling her simple cotton nightie over her head, past full breasts, slim abdomen and hips. Jake would hop out of bed and yank on his boxers before opening the door to scoop his sleepy rug rat into his arms. For the sake of his daydream he'd call the kid Mark, and he would smell a little sweaty and of cedar shavings—not unlike his pet hamster.

In his mind's eye, Jake watched himself lug Mark to their bed where he'd wriggle—footie pajamas and all—smack-dab into the middle before promptly falling asleep, snoring loud enough to wake the dead. And then, in milky moonlight, Candy would reach out to him, her husband and best friend, grasp his hand and give it a light squeeze. Without either of them saying a word, Jake would know his every wish had quietly come true.

Back to reality, Jake swallowed hard.

What happened, Candy? What happened between us to make love not be enough?

"Pizza should be here in about forty minutes."

He looked up.

Even doing something as simple as crossing the room, Candy had such grace. A long time ago she was everything he'd ever wanted and more. That long, silky hair, those even longer legs. When they made love, she'd had this way of wrapping those legs around him, urging him deeper, urging their souls closer, that had nearly made him weep with the sheer joy of being her man.

Now...

Whoa. Now, he just wanted out. Time to regroup.

The woman and her cozy kitchen were dangerous. "Forty minutes, huh? Whew, that's a long time."

"Yeah." At the waist of her simple floral dress, she fumbled with her hands. "Uh, want to watch a movie or something while we wait?"

"No, Candy, I think what we should do is talk."

Chapter Three

Minutes later, in the living room, Candy took the sofa while her ex choose an overstuffed tapestried wing chair.

Personally, she'd had enough talking, but seeing as how Jake probably wouldn't leave without spilling whatever was on his mind, she figured she might as well let him get it out of his system. "Okay," she said. "Let's hear it. What in the world made you re-propose this afternoon at the shop?"

"Jeez, where do I start?" He cleared his throat, worked the opening of his forest-green golf shirt—the one she was trying not to notice did such heavenly things with his annoyingly direct gaze. "I've gotten into a bit of a jam, and need your help—no, I'm desperate for your help." A strangled laugh passed his lips. "I would offer to pay you, but—"

"I get the picture. Go on."

"So anyway, I had these great friends, Cal and Jenny. And they had a great baby. Her name is Bonnie and you should see her blue eyes sparkle. I was at the hospital the day she was born—saw her just an hour out of the womb. Jenny told Cal all babies have blue eyes, but he told her, 'Nonsense, this beautiful kid of ours is destined to have the most striking pair of bonny blue peepers in the whole wide world.' And so they named her Bonnie Blue, just like Rhett and Scarlett's daughter—only I'll be damned if I ever let her near a horse.''

Candy leaned forward, spellbound by the change in Jake's expression. His eyes glowed with love for this child who wasn't even his. If there'd ever been a doubt in her mind that she hadn't done the right thing in giving him a divorce, it was gone now. Jake was destined to be a dad. Just like she was destined to never be a mom.

''In fact, I'm thinking of banning her from all moving things. Trikes, bikes, and especially cars—not to mention the wild teens who drive them.''

''Jake,'' she said, a sickening suspicion forming in her stomach. ''Why are you talking about this baby as if she's yours?''

He swallowed hard, and it was then she saw tears shimmer in his deep brown eyes. ''Because she *is* mine, Candy. Cal and Jenny—they died.''

''Oh, no.'' She flung her hand to her mouth. ''I'm sorry. So sorry.'' Not thinking, just doing, she went to him, wrapping him in a hug. ''How? They must have been so young.''

''Drunk driver,'' he said when she sat on the coffee table in front of him. ''It was bad. A couple of kids out cruising on a Friday night hit them head-on. Cops said the driver must've downed at least ten beers for his blood alcohol to be so—''

He paused to swallow, catch his breath, and she reached for his hand. "Go on. It's okay."

Nodding, he said, "Sorry. It's been a month, but it's still hard."

"I can imagine. These people were your friends."

"Yeah. They were the best. When my dad died, and then my mom, they were the ones who helped me through."

"I'm sorry I couldn't be there for your mom's funeral." She squeezed his hand. "But with Grandpa in the hospital last spring and everything."

"It's okay. I understood. I wish the guys down at the store would've told me he was sick. I'm sure he needed you."

I wanted you *to need me, too.*

Had she? Lord, what was happening? All of her carefully constructed emotional dams felt dotted with holes.

"Anyway," he said after expelling a deep breath. "In the emergency room, right after Jenny died, Cal asked me to take Bonnie. All they had for family was each other and their friends, so Cal asked me to raise their daughter like she was my own. And, of course, I agreed, never thinking it would actually come to that. But then Cal died, too. So…I did as he asked. And I've been caring for Bonnie ever since."

"Of course."

"And everything was going great. I was really getting the hang of the whole diaper thing and feeding. Bonnie's a good baby. At first, she cried a lot, but she seems to be getting better. She's known me her whole life, so I guess I'm making an all right substitute dad.''

"I know you, Jake. I'm sure you're making an awesome dad."

"Thanks."

"You're welcome."

"Problem is," he said, scratching his head, "Bonnie's great-aunt—a bitter old woman named Elizabeth Mannford—doesn't think so."

"Why?"

He gave her the short version of Mrs. Starling's speech. "So there you have it. My only hope of keeping Bonnie with the only family she knows is by getting hitched. And not just to anyone, Candy…but to you."

"Wow." Head spinning, Candy abruptly stood and put her hand to her forehead. "So that proposal of yours was the real deal? You truly do want to get married?"

He nodded. "But only until the adoption is legal. I'm figuring it'll take a year tops. In fact, after you make a brief appearance at Mrs. Starling's office, where we can dazzle her with our marriage license, rings and smiles—not to mention the old photo albums of how much fun we had back when we first got married—you'll probably be off the hook."

Candy, nibbling her pinkie fingernail, began to pace. Fireplace to breakfront. Breakfront to fireplace. "You know my family history, Jake. I vowed a long time ago to *never* be a mom. Do you know what you're asking?"

She paused just long enough to see him nod.

Fireplace to breakfront. "I mean, if I say no, that pretty much makes me the most heartless soul alive. Yet if I say yes, all my promises to myself…my plans… You don't know what it's been like for me since losing Grandpa. This is a small town. I'm surrounded by people who love me, yet I feel lost, like there's something missing inside of me I haven't been able to find. This trip, it means everything to me, Jake. It's about reclaiming my soul."

"So why can't you reschedule?"

"It's not that easy. The tour's being led by a top writer from *National Geographic*. I applied for the honor of being in her party almost a year ago. All the documentation on the sale of Candy Kisses has been finalized. I mean, my life is like the space shuttle, ready to blast off."

His expression dark, Jake stood. "So your answer is no. That's all you had to say. I understand."

"No. I mean, no, wait. That isn't my answer. I just need time to think. You showing up, throwing me this curve ball, it's all too much."

"I'm sorry, Candy. If I could, I'd give you all the time in the world. Jeez, if it were up to me, I wouldn't even be here. I'd just as soon tie the knot again as I would leap off a cliff."

"Thanks. Glad to know how much you enjoy my company."

"You know what I mean. It's not like getting married was my idea. Anyway, bottom line, I can give you a week, but that's it. If I'm not back in Florida by then, who knows what this Elizabeth Mannford may do. I wouldn't put it past her to charge me with kidnapping.''

"Okay, then," Candy said, fingering long strands of her hair. "A week it is. I'll give you my answer Saturday night at the reunion.''

FROM WHERE SHE SAT cross-legged on Candy's sofa, Kelly snagged a piece of sausage-and-mushroom pizza, brought it to her lips and groaned. "Five delicious pounds in the smell alone.''

Candy summoned a weak smile. "Thanks for coming over. Jake left so suddenly, I was at a loss as to what to do next.''

"Candy," Kelly said, slapping her friend lightly on the back. "You called the right person, because faced with an entire pizza, believe me, I know just what to do.''

"Not about the pizza," Candy said. "About Jake. I feel so torn. Like I have to help him, but at the same time, like there's no way I can help him. It took me such a long time to get over him, how can I possibly go through the whole thing again?''

"It's not as if he wants to get married for real.''

"I know, but his plan sounds like a pretty dangerous emotional game.''

"So don't play it." Kelly sipped at a cola.

"But if I don't, I'll feel like a schmuck.''

"So do it.''

"Gee, thanks," Candy said, shooting her friend a dirty look. "You're a ton of help.''

"Look, the guy gave you a week to think it over,

why do you have to decide in the next thirty minutes?''

Candy swigged her own cola. ''Because that's who I am. I'm legendary in the shop's kitchen for being quick on my feet in times of crisis. I mean, any time we run out of unsweetened chocolate, who else but me is going to know you can substitute unsweetened cocoa powder plus butter? And did you know one and a quarter cups granulated sugar plus a quarter cup of any liquid also works? And that if you run out of cake flour, then—''

''News flash,'' Kelly said through trailing mozzarella. ''We're not in your boring old shop kitchen. This is real life, Candy. And guess what?''

''What?''

''Sometimes it sucks.''

''Gee, Kel, that's sweet. Have you ever considered a second career writing greeting cards?''

''I'M COMING, I'm coming.'' At six o'clock Tuesday morning, eyes barely open, Candy felt her way down the stairs and to the front door.

Whoever stood outside rang the doorbell again.

She growled before asking, ''Who is it?''

''Me.''

Jake. Oh, now that woke her right up. She flew her hands to her face, hair, thin white tank T-shirt and cat print pajama bottoms. ''Go away!''

''Why?''

''I'm not dressed.''

She swore she heard him chuckle. ''Come on, Candy, it's not like I haven't seen it all before.''

It had been on the tip of her tongue to reply with a sassy, "Yeah, but you haven't seen mine," when her conscience chose to remind just how much of her he *had* seen.

The last time they'd made love—not long before she'd asked him for a divorce—had been right there in the living room, on the couch she told Jake she'd taken to the dump. Good thing she'd had the foresight to move Goldilocks into the boathouse, or he might have gotten the wrong idea—like she held a soft spot for the wretched thing. And God forbid he actually think she'd enjoyed all those nights with him spent rolling around on that couch.

Her cheeks burned.

Okay, so maybe I enjoyed just a few of those nights.

And that last night... Oh, that last night had been steamy in every possible way....

Rain had been falling in driving sheets. That summer, Lonesome had been going through a drought, and the air that night was ripe—smelling of parched earth taking a good, long drink. Since they hadn't been able to afford air-conditioning, the humidity had had them glowing with sweat. They'd been watching TV, but about nine-thirty they'd turned it off, planning to take a quick shower before hitting the sack. With only the one lamp on and the occasional strobe of lightning, the living room had been nearly dark.

"Come here," Jake had said from the sofa.

"Why? I thought we were going to bed."

He'd shaken his head, wielded that slow, sexy grin that melted her like butter. "Come here, gorgeous."

She remarked that her heart had pounded just looking at her handsome husband, stretched out on the couch wearing only black boxers and his hard-earned muscles. Her mouth had gone so dry. Other parts of her—lower parts—had dampened with need.

"Peel off your shirt."

"Here?"

"No, in the kitchen." He'd shot her another slow grin. "Damn straight, *here.* I want to see my merchandise...."

The doorbell ding-donged three times.

"Come on, Candy! I brought breakfast and the groceries are getting heavy!"

Pulse pounding, palms sweating, Candy licked her lips. Opening the door, she averted her gaze, scared to death Jake could tell just by looking at her exactly what she'd been thinking.

"Morning, gorgeous. Mmm, it sure smells better in here than it did last night with all those corn dogs flaming. Miss me?" He kissed her on the forehead before strolling in. Even worse, it wasn't groceries he carried, but the most adorable pink-cheeked, blue-eyed baby she'd ever seen.

Her heart lurched.

"Bonnie," he said, turning the infant away from his chest and toward her. "Meet Candy. Hopefully, she'll agree to be your temporary mom." To Candy he said, "Wanna hold her?"

"Uh, no thanks." Arms crossed, she shook her head—just in case there was something about her verbal message he hadn't understood. Even from a good two feet away, she detected distinctly disturbing baby scents. Baby lotion, baby shampoo, baby powder—

even Bonnie's ruffled pink dress sported the annoyingly pleasant scent of laundry detergent. From a safe distance—say, ten feet—all of those smells were nice enough, but up close and personal? No. Couldn't happen.

Except for that one time you've never told anyone about.

Yes, but I've already established the fact that an incident like that will never happen again!

Candy knew better. Babies were toxic to her system, and if she wasn't careful, she might end up suffering some kind of meltdown. Frowning, she said, "Have you ever heard of picking up a phone?"

He grinned. "I couldn't remember the number."

"Lonesome does have phone books."

"Yeah, but lucky for me, it also has rental cars, so I figured, what the hey? I might as well drive over."

"Sure. Why not."

"Great. I'm glad you're happy to see us. Here," he said, thrusting out the baby. "Take her while I carry in the grub."

"Jake, I—" Too late, the infant was already in her arms.

"Abba, blabba—goo!" The tiny creature giggled. *Wow. Oh, wow.*

To relieve tension, Candy would have ordinarily twirled a couple hundred hanks of hair, but seeing how at the moment her hands were kind of full, all she could do was stare at the wide open, porcelain-blue gaze staring at her.

"So," she said. "You're Bonnie. I've heard a lot about you."

"Bzzzzz." A few bubbles escaped lips so perfectly round and sweet, they resembled a big, fat cherry plopped into the midst of Bonnie's whipped-cream-smooth complexion.

The child gave a few sharp kicks before, with a juicy sigh, snuggling against Candy's breasts.

Over her years spent working in a candy store, Candy had been coerced into holding her share of babies, but somehow, knowing this was Jake's baby—even if by horrible tragedy as opposed to her being of his flesh and blood—made the experience different.

Better, in a terrifying way.

"Jake!" she hollered out the door. "Hurry!"

"What's the problem?" he called, just the top of his heartstoppingly handsome mug visible above the paper sacks with Gregg's Grocery emblazoned across the side.

Candy peered at the angel resting her cheek on her left breast. *Problem? Gee, where do I start?* "Uh, well, I think—"

"How cute. I think that means she likes you."

"Yes, well…"

"You two hang out while I cook."

"But I really…"

He'd shut the front door and headed for the kitchen.

"…don't think this is going to work." On her own again with Bonnie, Candy made a beeline for the kitchen. "Come on, Jake, you know about me and babies. Unless someone practically forces me to hold an infant down at the store, I always steer clear. My friends don't even let me baby-sit."

"Have you ever offered?" he asked, unloading bacon, eggs, cheese and…chili?

"Well…" Bonnie wriggled, repositioning herself so that tufts of her fluffy blond hair tickled Candy's chin. A second later the baby's mini hair bow slid to the floor. Candy knelt to pick it up, then, as efficiently as possible while working one-handed, she brushed the pink scrap against her flannel PJ bottoms. Wouldn't do for Bonnie to get dust in her hair. Bow neatly back in place, Candy said, "I don't suppose I ever volunteered, but then, everybody knows I'm no good with babies. I mean, besides my indestructible goldfish, I don't even have any pets."

"We had that kitten."

"Dabney?" Heart aching from the memory of the tiny kitten, and the brief joy it had brought into their lives, Candy gave Bonnie a slight squeeze. "If I ever had another cat, I'd make her an inside cat. That way nothing could happen to it."

She looked up to see Jake frown.

"What? You think a lawn service truck is going to come barreling through the living room?"

"No, it's just that if there's anything I've learned over the past month, it's that nothing's permanent. I mean, we can think it is, but jeez, when I remember how one minute Cal and Jenny were with me at a late dinner meeting, and the next…"

Cupping her palm to the curve of Bonnie's head, Candy pressed her lips to impossibly sweet-smelling hair. Poor little thing.

"Guess what I'm getting at is that stuff happens. All we can do is live for the moment and hope for the best. So," he said, looking as if he was making an effort to lighten his expression. "How about one of my world-famous, chili-cheese omelets?"

ALL THROUGH BREAKFAST, Jake watched.

Bonnie with Candy. Candy with Bonnie.

And all through breakfast, one thing became abundantly clear: Candy would make a great temporary mom. If only he could convince her of that fact.

In the brief time he'd been there, he'd already seen dozens of positive signs. Sure, at first, she'd been tentative about the whole baby thing, but no doubt about it, she was softening. The squeezes, the kisses pressed to Bonnie's forehead, the unconscious yet meticulous care taken with repositioning her hair bow. Could the morning's plans be proceeding any more smoothly?

In fact, things were running so smoothly, that in the living room, Bonnie had even sacked out in the portable playpen Jake had brought in from the car. Nothing—and he meant *nothing*—was more irresistible than sleeping Bonnie. She was so cute that he wouldn't be surprised to find Miss I-Don't-Care-For-Babies sneaking in there for a few quick rump pats!

"That was good," Candy said, pushing her empty plate aside to make room for a cup of coffee. "At first, I have to admit to having doubts about your creation, but now I bow to your omelet prowess."

"Thanks. I perfected these babies on the last company camp-a-thon."

"Camp-a-thon?"

"Yeah. Me and the other board members get people to sponsor us to camp on the roof of Galaxy

Sports headquarters. It's grown into a pretty big deal—customers drive by, honking at us and dropping off cash donations. This year, we raised a bundle for Special Olympics.''

Grinning, Candy said, ''Why doesn't it surprise me that you don't host simple, black-tie, fund-raising dinners like other business tycoons?''

''What's the fun in that? I mean, come on, how many CEOs do you know who get to spend a whole week sleeping under the stars and playing rooftop volleyball all in the name of charity?''

''You've got a point there.''

Inside, Jake couldn't help but preen. Candy's improved mood could only mean one thing. Not only had he seduced her with his cooking, but she'd seen what a love bug Bonnie was and didn't even need the rest of the week to decide to remarry him. A fact that put him in the mood to party. ''Say, Candy Cane, if you don't have anything going on today, how about we head down to the lake for a sail?''

She choked on her latest sip of coffee.

Good sign or bad? Man, oh, man, what had gotten into him to have accidentally called her ''Candy Cane''?

''That sounds nice,'' she said, ''but I have to pack. And this afternoon, I should head over to the shop. I want to make sure there's a surplus of everything when the new owners take charge. They're friends. Greg and Betsy Hammond. Remember them from high school? They were a grade ahead of us.''

''Sure. How are they?''

''Good. Betsy just had their fourth boy. I think she

was hoping for a girl this time, but…'' Fidgeting with her hands, she said, ''Anyway, they're about the only ones happy with my decision to sell. Kelly's finally cutting me some slack, but when I first told her, she read me the riot act.''

''So why are you doing it? I mean, why take such a drastic step as to outright sell? Why not leave it in the hands of your most trusted employees? Surely someone could run the place while you take time off?''

Head bowed, Candy said, ''It's not that simple. I need the money to travel, and I'm afraid what I'm looking for can't be found in a few days. Something's missing inside me, Jake.'' Palms pressed to her chest, she said, ''I feel lonely in crowds, like there's a piece of me out there that I haven't been able to find. I *have* to take this trip. I'm sorry if my selling Candy Kisses hurts people's feelings. It's hurting me, too. That business is my only family aside from you—or, I mean, at least you *used* to be my family. Now…'' She flopped her hands on her lap. ''I don't know, I just feel restless.''

At first, Jake thought every word his ex muttered about needing to find herself had been hogwash, but now, seeing the sadness in Candy's eyes, made the part of him that would always care about her wonder if maybe she was on the right track. Because, shoot, who was he to say running off on some great adventure wouldn't be the key to unlocking whatever tormented her soul?

Problem was, if Candy took off to find her soul, that left him losing his. For if the state took Bonnie,

Jake knew he'd be done for. Oh, no matter how bad it hurt, he'd abide by the law and give her up, but doing so might very well kill him.

Toying with his coffee cup, Jake said, "I don't mean to pressure you, Candy, but I can't begin to explain how much Bonnie means to me. I can't—"

"No, Jake. Don't do this. Please don't play the guilt card. It isn't fair." Candy pushed back her chair, reached for their plates, and stormed to the sink.

Jake followed suit.

At the sink, he spun her around to face him. "Mind telling me what is fair? You can go on this trip of yours anytime. I'm not asking you to cancel flat-out, just to postpone. If you want to be stupid enough to throw away a business that has the potential to one day become a family legacy like Hershey or Godiva, be my guest. All I'm asking for is a year—maybe even less—of your time."

"Oh, that's great," she said, hurling the scrub sponge into the sink. "Now you're calling me stupid?"

"Not *you,* your decision. It's rash. Not at all like you."

"How do you even know me? Since you followed your folks to Florida when they retired, it's been ten years since we've really talked. Sure, I saw you at your dad's funeral a few years back, but that was different. It didn't count. For all practical purposes, we might as well be strangers."

Strangers? Was she listening to her own words?

Not thinking, just doing, Jake pulled her into his arms and pressed his lips against hers in a desperate attempt to see that if he couldn't talk sense into her, then at least maybe he could kiss it into her.

At first, she went stiff—undoubtedly from shock. But then she softened, molded herself to his chest, his arms.

Years cracked and then slipped away, and it was as if their bodies had never been apart. Trapped heat grew and swirled.

Closer. Jake wanted closer. No, not just close— inside. He wanted all of her.

Now.

As they used to be.

Was he only dreaming, or was her pulse pounding in time with his?

The dream ended when Candy, hands covering swollen lips, eyes glowing whiskey-brown daze, pushed him away. "I'm sorry, Jake. I can't."

"Can't what? It was just a kiss."

Candy squeezed her eyes shut. *No, Jake. That's where you're wrong. That wasn't a mere kiss, but an opening to the door I've worked years to shut.* Legs, hands and heart trembling, Candy said with all the conviction she could muster, "I—I think you'd better leave."

Chapter Four

"Now here's where I think you're going about this all wrong," Dietz said. The brawny guy with hair the color of a Viking you'd nickname Eric the Red managed the team sport section of Jake's Lonesome store.

"Oh, boy, here it comes," Rick and Warren said in unison, rolling their eyes. They'd sprawled their legs so far out in front of them that they resembled a couple of pumped-up Raggedy Andy dolls a child had carelessly flopped onto folding metal chairs.

Jake assumed that, like him, they were near passing out from eating too much of Warren's wife's lasagna. Damn, it'd been good, and the sweet basil and tomato scent of the sauce still lingered in the ugly but comfortable break room.

As much as he tried fighting the sensation, being back at his first store, with his first friends, Jake was filled with the same sense of belonging he'd felt that morning in Candy's kitchen—at least he had felt as though he'd belonged until she'd asked him to leave.

Bonnie was again sacked out, this time in a nest of pillows on the break room's sagging brown sofa.

While Jake laughed, Dietz flipped his co-workers a good-natured bird. ''As I was saying. Our boy here's taking a completely wrong course of action. I say he ignore Candy all together. Maybe even ask Amanda Perkins and her brand new Double Ds to the reunion—that'll for sure get Candy's goat.''

During Dietz's formative years, he'd been labeled the bad boy of Lonesome High. As such, he'd been dumped by more cheerleaders than the school mascot Jimmy Gooligan. But since Jimmy had formed the top of wobbly cheer pyramids and had been dressed in a slippery blue Falcon suit, his dumpings didn't really count.

Dietz, on the other hand, had been dumped the hard way, meaning not even by the hot girls he'd dated, but by their shotgun-wielding daddies. As a result, Dietz now came across as the James Dean wounded-hero type. Not intentionally planning to hurt anyone, Dietz somehow managed to foul up good relationships before they had a chance to foul him up.

''You know, though,'' Warren said, sliding upright in his chair, ''Dietz might not have such a bad idea. Example from my own extensive relationship files—''

''What relationships?'' Rick cracked. ''You and Franny been going together since junior high, then got married right out of high school.''

''Hey,'' Warren said, ''I might only have been with one woman, but believe you me, she's as complex as they come.''

Rick again rolled his eyes.

"Go on, Warren," Jake said. "At this point, I'm open to any and all suggestions."

Looking vindicated, Warren continued. "One thing I know about my Franny, is that if there's ever anything I want her to do, I ask her to do the opposite—just like she did to me on this house deal."

Face scrunched, Jake said, "Come again?"

"Okay, maybe if I draw it out for you it'll be easier to understand." Warren headed up space planning for the store and tended to diagram most conversations. Lunging across the table for Dietz's brown paper lunch sack, he pressed it flat, then used the pen from his shirt pocket to sketch his house.

"Here's me," he said, pointing to the stick figure in front of the crooked garage. "Note the busted garage door."

"Look's all right to me," Dietz said.

"Yeah, well it's not," Rick said. "You should hear the motor on that thing. Whines like a stuck baby pig."

Now it was Jake's turn to roll his eyes. "Can you two duke this out some other time while Warren here gets on with his lesson?"

Warren drew what Jake assumed was Stick Franny on the front porch. She had a cruel slash for a mouth and beady dot eyes. "Note my wife, glaring at me for even suggesting we spend our tax refund on what she calls a perfectly good garage door when we could blow it on new carpet. Now, what I did just this morning was tell her she's right. We should definitely buy new carpet, because if she's even thinking about selling the house and buying a bigger one this summer, then potential buyers are going to care a whole lot more about new carpet than a cranky old garage door that decides whether it'll open or not depending on its mood.''

"Ah," Dietz said. "I get it. Reverse psychology. Wonder if Amanda would fall for it?"

"I thought Amanda was going to be *my* date?" Jake teased.

"Yeah, well, now that Warren told you what to do, you can go back to finding your own date."

TUESDAY AFTERNOON after closing the shop, Candy headed across the back lot toward her trusty sky-blue minivan only to get a shock.

There was Jake—Bonnie contentedly cooing in a carrier at his feet—stepping out from behind the van's rear window.

"Oh, hey," he said, blasting her with his sexiest slow grin. He wiped his hands on the thighs of his faded jeans. "I was just putting on a new rear-window wiper blade for you. I did the front, too. Did you know the rubber was so old it was actually cracked?"

"Of course, I knew," she said, crossing her fingers behind her back to ward off bad fibbing karma. "I, uh, just haven't had time to change the wipers myself."

Nodding, he said, "Sure, that's what I figured."

"Well…thanks," she said, twirling a lock of hair, being extra careful not to cross into Bonnie's baby scent zone. "So? What are you doing here? Besides working on my car?"

He knelt to unfasten the baby then zoom her giggling through the air before blowing a raspberry on one cheek, kissing the other, and tucking her into his arms. "I just stopped by for a quick chat."

"Why didn't you come into the shop?"

"I almost did, but I saw you were busy and what I have to say is best said in private."

"Oh." Her stomach knotted. Here came another pressure-filled *Marry Me* speech.

"Pretty day, isn't it? And I'd forgotten how good old Digger's Barbecue smells when he fires up his smoker for the dinner crowd."

"I hadn't noticed," she said. Just like she hadn't noticed anything or anyone since he'd waltzed back into her life.

"You should," he said, trading Bonnie to his other arm. The movement was just enough to stir breathless air, assailing Candy with those dastardly baby scents. Shouldn't there be some kind of legislation about the alluring fragrance of baby lotions and shampoo?

"It's gotta be eighty out here," he said, "and did you ever see such a dazzling blue sky?"

In Bonnie's big blue eyes.

Candy frowned, hastily looking away from the tantalizing pink bundle. "No—I mean, yes. You've just been away too long. We have this kind of sky all year long." In what was starting to be a habit, she caught herself crossing her fingers again, adding Jake's muscled forearms to her list of prohibited views. They were tanned—just like the rest of him—and the hair glinted gold in the warm sun.

''Remember what we used to do on days like this?''

''Uh, no…'' she said, having not even bothered to uncross her fingers from her last fib. As memories crept into her heart, heat washed her cheeks.

As newlyweds, most every spring weekend they'd hiked hand in hand through the age-old Missouri forest.

One particularly spellbinding day, they'd rested beside a bubbling stream, then climbed atop moss-covered boulders to lie like turtles soaking in the hot sun.

Candy would never forget the feel of that sun or the way slanted sunbeams had cast lacy shadows through a canopy of tender spring leaves. Rich soil and cool running water had flavored the air with damp sweetness, and somewhere among the myriad of branches, a jay had called to his mate.

Just when Candy had thought catching sight of Mother Nature herself couldn't make the moment more special, Jake had risen onto his elbow and gazed into her eyes with such fire she'd thought she'd surely die from the sheer range and crushing intensity of emotions. Desire. And fear that the magic they shared couldn't last. Wonder. And awe that they'd even lasted that long. Above all else, love, and the devil-may-care attitude of the naive young that for however long Jake would have her, Candy would be his.

Trailing his big hand along her abdomen, he'd pushed up her T-shirt. Undone the button on her jeans cutoffs, easing down the zipper nice and slow. She'd always been too shy for a bikini and the hot sun on her tummy stroked her with wild, forbidden heat.

Without breaking his stare, Jake had reached for a dandelion, tickling it up and over the gentle swell of her belly, tracing the fine line of hair leading into her panties.

"The sight of you takes my breath away," he'd said.

"Sorry," she'd answered, not knowing whether to giggle or cry from happiness.

"You should be sorry," he'd teased. "You should also be kissed."

Just when she'd closed her eyes in anticipation of feeling his lips pressed against hers, he'd surprised her by blowing a raspberry on her tummy....

Jake, pretending not to notice Candy's dreamy expression, lifted Bonnie high, then on her trip down, blew a raspberry on the strip of her belly peeking between pink shorts and T-shirt. Could that la-la-land daze in his ex-wife's eyes mean she remembered more of their past than she let on?

"Anyway," he said, swinging Bonnie onto his shoulders, holding her firm against his head with one hand while with the other he held her feet. "I came here to apologize for last night."

"Oh?" She was back to twirling her hair.

"I had no right to ask you to marry me—and I sure as hell had no right to kiss you. It was a mistake, and I'm sorry. I promise, it will never happen again."

"I see." She'd added nibbling her lower lip to her hair-twirling routine. Hmm, that was some talent she had going there. Kind of like walking and chewing gum.

"In fact," he said, "I was planning to stay for the reunion, but now I'm thinking it'd probably be best for you if Bonnie and I went home."

"What about Elizabeth Mannford?"

He shrugged, glancing up at the baby when she rested her cheek on his head. Her pudgy hands gripped his eyebrows. "I guess the best I can hope for is that she'll see how much we love each other— me and Bonnie, that is—and have a change of heart."

"Sure." Candy halted all twirling and nibbling to cross her arms. "I suppose that makes sense."

"I don't mean to keep you," Jake said, "but I did have one more thing to ask."

"What's that?"

"Have dinner with me tonight? I'm sure I can get Warren and Franny to watch Bonnie. I feel lousy about last night and want to make it up to you. You know, leave town on a high note."

"Sure, uh, I guess that would be okay."

"Great. I'll pick you up at seven. Oh, and…here, hold Bonnie for a sec while I jot down the number of where I'm staying."

"No, I don't need—" Too late. Jake had already put Bonnie into her arms. "A number."

"Sure you do. In case something comes up."

Feeling a warm puff of milky-smelling baby breath against her cheek, Candy froze. *Oh, something's coming up all right, Jake. My panic over once again holding your baby!*

This simply wouldn't do.

Yes, his leaving town with this fragrant pink bundle would be best for everyone involved.

What about Bonnie? Would it best for her to have Jake snatched away just as cruelly as her parents?

"Here you go," Jake said, handing her his business card with a number scribbled on the back. "I'm staying at the Oak Lodge out on Highway 248."

"Honestly, Jake, you could've just told me the name of your motel. I know how to use a phone book."

"You're right. Why didn't I think of that?"

"Probably because this was a trick, and you're not really planning on going home at all. You just wanted me to hold Bonnie again. To see how cute she is and how good she smells."

"You're wrong, Candy. I wouldn't do that."

"Oh, you wouldn't, huh? Not even to keep Bonnie?"

Hands to his chest, he said, "That hurts. Do you really have such a low opinion of me that you think I'd stoop to not only manipulating you with mind games, but using a poor, defenseless baby to do it?" He reached for the infant, catching Candy off guard at the pang she felt upon letting Bonnie go.

"All right," Candy said, blaming the short-lived pang on Jake-induced guilt. She was still wary of the motive behind his dinner invitation, but she had a few motives of her own—such as wanting to convince herself that his kiss hadn't been all that great. That her heart still didn't gallop every time her mind whispered his name. Once and for all, she needed to get the message through that thick skull of hers that she was over him. "I'll go to dinner with you tonight, but only under one condition."

"What?"

"That you promise you're going home tomorrow."

"Promise," Jake said, hiding his crossed fingers well behind Bonnie's diaper-clad behind.

"SHOULD I WEAR the red or black?" Candy asked Kelly at six-thirty. Standing in front of her bedroom closet, she wagged the two dresses at her friend.

"Just a minute," Kelly mumbled from behind her soap opera magazine. "Let me finish this paragraph."

"Honestly, why did I even ask you over?"

"That's easy." From where she was lounging on her stomach across the foot of the dress-strewn bed, Kelly peered over the top of her page and grinned. "Because deep down, you still have a thing for Jake, but since you're knee-deep in denial, you need me around to remind you."

Candy snatched a ruffled yellow pillow from the head of the bed and flung it at her so-called friend. "Again, thanks for nothing."

"Sure. Any time." Easily having dodged the pillow, the blonde returned to her reading.

"*Kelly?* Help! He's going to be here in twenty-five minutes."

With a big sigh, Kelly slapped her magazine onto the bed, then pushed herself to an upright position. "You want my opinion—you're trying entirely too hard. You pour yourself into either the red or black, he's gonna know you want him way more than some twelve ninety-nine steak platter."

"But I don't want him."

"So you say."

"Kelly," Candy warned.

"Okay, so for the sake of this conversation, let's just say you don't want to kiss him, lick him or even like him. Then I vote you wear jeans and a T-shirt."

"I can't do that," Candy said. "That would send him the message that I was trying too hard *not* to impress him, which would then lead to him thinking I really do want to impress him."

"There you go," Kelly said, once again reaching for her magazine. "You answered your own question."

Twirling her hair, Candy said, "You're right, I should definitely wear the red."

"COME ON, JAKE," Candy said when he parked his rental sedan at the entrance to Lonesome High's Falcon Field. "This isn't funny. Where are we really going?" Sure, she'd finally put their past behind her, but knowing the special time the two of them shared in this very spot, she thought his joke was in poor taste.

He turned off the engine, angling on the navy leather seat to face her. "Who said I was trying to be funny?"

"Then why are we here?"

His smile faded, eyes darkened. "You don't remember? Our first date?"

"Of course I remember our first date. But what does that have to do with tonight?"

"Everything," he said, taking her hands in his. Had

she not been long over him, the sensation of his warm fingers cocooning hers could have reduced her to an old-fashioned swoon. As it was, her heart started up again with that disconcerting gallop and her breaths came shallow—if at all. ''I want tonight to be a fresh start for us,'' he said. ''I want the bitterness of our divorce behind us so that if we can't be lovers...'' With the pads of his thumbs, he brushed the sides of her index fingers, strumming an erotic storm in areas of her body she'd long since forgotten. ''At the very least, I'd like us to be friends.''

''That, uh, sounds nice,'' she said, tugging her lower lip into her mouth for a quick nibble. ''But there's an awful lot of history between us, Jake. Are we supposed to ignore all of that?''

''For tonight.''

''And tomorrow?''

''Tomorrow, Bonnie and I will be gone.''

''What about her custody case?''

''I'll handle it when the time comes. Believe me, no one regrets my asking you to marry me again more than me. I mean, I must've gone temporarily stupid to have ever even considered such a screwball scheme working.''

''Oh, I don't know,'' she said, licking her lips when he finally released her hands. ''The idea had merit. It just wouldn't have worked with me—at least not now. I mean, maybe if you'd come some other time...''

''Then you might have considered it?''

''Well, no, but...'' She fanned herself with her red

envelope purse. "Whew, my goodness, is it just me, or did it turn warm in here?"

His eyes.

When they'd been married, how had she finished a single thought peering into their velvety depths? With each passing moment, she feared drowning in the tropical spice of Jake's aftershave and the hint of mint on his breath.

"I suppose it is a little warm. Ready to get down to business?"

"Business?"

"Yeah," he said with a wide grin. "You know, the business of our date?"

"This isn't a date. I thought we were just eating dinner?"

"You're right. Anyway, come on. I've got a special night planned." He held out his hand for her before opening his door, then urged her to scoot out his side instead of her own. As she slid across his seat, much to her dismay she found the leather had retained his heat, which now soaked through the flimsy silk of her dress. For the briefest of seconds, she was returned to the memory of how it used to feel to dance with Jake's hands cupping her— No!

No cupping, no dancing, and especially no more heat!

Tonight was merely a friendly goodbye dinner.

Nothing more.

Unfortunately for Candy, though, standing outside with Jake rummaging in the trunk, the air didn't feel much cooler than it had in the car, but at least the scent of the freshly mown football field rescued her from once again falling victim to Jake's aftershave.

Thank goodness he was going home tomorrow, because she sincerely doubted her ability to keep a firm hold on her sanity being around him even one more hour!

What was wrong with her?

Why did she keep forgetting that in less than a week, she would embark on the most amazing adventure of her life? And why was it she suddenly feared rafting over Niagara Falls wouldn't make her heart race the way it did when Jake gifted her with just one of his lazy smiles?

RECLINING on the fifty-yard line with Candy beside him and a winking galaxy above, Jake should have felt like a million bucks. Trouble was, after downing two ham sandwiches, almost a full bag of Cheetos, and a half dozen Chips Ahoy! cookies, he hadn't gotten Candy anywhere close to asking him to stay. She had pointed out however, that if his intention had been to recreate their first date, then he'd gotten their meal wrong.

Little did she know that wasn't the only thing he'd gotten wrong! How could he have let Warren and Dietz talk him into such an asinine plan?

Even worse, was the sight of Candy stretched out beside him, her candy-apple-red dress hugging her full breasts and hips about as well as his red Maserati hugged winding roads. In other words, the sight of her in that dress caused major below-the-belt havoc— making him damned glad he didn't have to share her with anyone but the singing crickets.

She'd piled her long dark hair high and the evening's heat and humidity loosened neck-kissing tendrils. An irrational streak of jealousy stormed him. He wanted to be the one kissing her neck!

"How is it," he said, "that you claim to not remember that awesome blue bow tie I wore to the prom, but you do remember that we had turkey on rye for our first date, and Fritos—not Cheetos?"

"Easy," she said, sucking orange Cheetos crumbs from the tips of her thumb and index finger. "I remember quite clearly you saying how you'd read in your sister's *Cosmo* that turkey and rye made girls hot—kind of like green M&M's."

After flicking a fallen Cheetos her way, he rolled his eyes. "Yeah, right. There's no way in hell I said something like that. Especially not back then when my cool factor was off the charts."

She laughed hard enough to choke on a swig of cola.

Jake, however, failed to see the humor in the situation, especially when watching her sweet lips curve around her fingers had given him the craziest urge to recreate the ending of their first date.

The part where he rolled on top of her, kissed her until, her expression dazed, she'd asked him if that meant they were going together. Young, dumb, and full of— Well, anyway, he'd said yes. Officially asked her to be his girl, and they'd been together ever since. Or rather, they *would* have still been together if her hang-up over having kids hadn't forced them apart.

"What's the matter?" she asked, realizing she was laughing alone.

He shook his head. "Nothing. I guess all this reminiscing makes me a little sad."

"How so?"

"Oh, I don't know, just thinking back to how happy we used to be. How much hope we held in store for our future. But then how our lives ultimately turned out—not that I'm complaining, just saying that my current path isn't quite what I had in mind."

"Yeah," Candy said, an almost wistful tone to her voice. "I know what you mean."

For a long time they shared a comfortable silence, staring up at the stars.

Closing his eyes, Jake recalled how cute Candy had looked twirling her baton across this very spot. How many football battles had he helped fight on this field? How many times had Candy celebrated with him afterward on this field, win or lose?

All those memories made him wish he would still be in town for their reunion. Sure, he knew how his closest friends' lives turned out, but what about the rest of their old crowd? "You mentioned your friend Kelly a little while ago. How's she doing?"

"She's all right. Still a swinging single."

"Any chance of us hooking her up with Dietz?"

"Are you kidding me? Those two dated a few years back and came close to killing each other. Believe me, the whole town is better off with them apart."

He laughed. "She was a cool girl. I'd hoped for a chance to see her before I left town."

"She likes you, too—only she'll get a real kick out

of hearing what we did tonight since she thinks our first date was bizarre.''

"So do Rick, Dietz and Warren. They thought I should have taken you into Springfield for a movie and McDonald's.''

"Kelly thought you should have taken me to the Springfield Red Lobster, then the mall.''

"What about you, Candy? What did you think?''

Fixing her gaze on the stars, she said, "The truth?''

"Duh.''

Even in the dark, he felt their gazes lock. "I thought ours was the perfect first date.''

Enfolding her hand in his, Jake softly said, "Me, too, Candy Cane. Me, too.''

Chapter Five

"That was nice," Candy said an hour later on her front porch, turning her key in the door lock. "Thank you. I—" She lowered her gaze. "I have to admit that when you first suggested going out tonight, I thought it was a pretty lame idea, but…"

He tucked his strong, warm fingers beneath her chin, dragging her gaze to his. "But I'm not as bad as you've made me out to be all these years?"

"Well…" She couldn't hold back an embarrassed giggle.

He laughed. "I feel the same, Candy—not that you're bad—but that my opinion of you has done a one-eighty." He stepped closer, closer, until the heat trapped between them made her lose track of why she was so all-fired eager to see him leave. He took her hands in his, gave them a light squeeze. "I'd forgotten that funny little snort you make when you laugh. And the way you always smell sweet—like a freshly opened box of chocolates."

"I don't snort," she said, setting the record straight. "And speaking of sweet," she added with a breathless grin. "You sure haven't lost your knack for sweet talk."

"I'm flattered you remember." Dropping his gaze, he scuffed the toe of his loafer across the porch floor. "Funny thing is, though, I haven't done much of it lately—say, like in the last ten years."

Oh, how Candy wanted to believe that. But with that line, he'd gone too far. Lonesome might not be the information capital of the world, but they did get all of the major magazines. Jake had been a *Cosmo* Bachelor of the Month for heaven's sake! And here he was expecting her to believe a cornball line like he'd never sweet-talked any woman but her? "You are some piece of work, Peterson."

"How so, Peterson?"

"I go by Jacobs now, thank you very much."

"Okay, *Jacobs,* how so?"

"Do you have any idea how many times I've seen you and some stacked Amazon princess appear arm in arm on the glossy pages of *Vanity Fair*?"

He shrugged. "Sorry, but that's not something I keep track of. Now, Galaxy Sports's latest sales figures, I've got back in my motel room, but if you've gotta have hard data on magazine appearances, you'll have to connect with my publicist." His expression was so earnest, so sincere, she almost believed him. Then his face cracked into that thoroughly annoying, damned sexy grin.

"I'm serious," she said, lightly smacking him on his arm, but not light enough to escape the feel of hard muscle beneath the thin cotton of his shirt. "It's not nice for you to say those things to me, when I know they're probably the same old lines you use on Bunny and Barbie and…and I don't know—Brandy!''

"Ah, yes," he said with a great look of wisdom. "The infamous BBB triplets. Dated them in March of 1998, I believe, then Brandy came down with chicken pox. Infected the whole crew. Damned spotty mess if you ask me. So then I moved on to the FFM triplets. Fluffy, Fern and Muffy.''

Candy smacked him again, but this time Jake grabbed her hand. "You may think everything I've said tonight was a joke, but I don't. When I said you have a cute snort in your laugh, I meant it. Ditto for you smelling like chocolates. Do you know how many women I date who reek of custom-mixed perfume that gives me a headache? You're different, Candy. I don't know…refreshing. You make me feel different. *Alive*.'' He gave her hand a squeeze. "Makes me glad Bonnie and I are going home.''

Candy wanted to say something. Truly, she did, but words stuck in her throat.

She made Jake feel alive?

Wow, that was funny, because now that he mentioned it, she felt the same way about him. Mortified by the discovery, she licked her lips.

Yes, it was a very good thing he was leaving. Hopefully, in the morning.

First thing in the morning.

That way she'd be safe in enjoying him for just a teensy bit longer tonight. Releasing his hand, she turned her attention back to inserting her key in the front door lock. "I don't suppose you want to come in for a quick bite of dessert?"

"You don't have any dessert," he said from somewhere behind her, close enough that his heat warmed her back.

"Oops. Guess you're right." Facing him, she planted herself against the door. "But I do have plenty of pickles, ketchup and mustard—oh, and all the stuff left over from this morning."

"Thanks," he said, "but after downing that sack of Chips Ahoy!, I'm not all that hungry. Plus, I really should be getting back to Bonnie, and I've yet to get hold of my pilot. Last time I spoke with him, he was flying a team of buyers to Beijing. I've tried him a couple times since, but I keep getting that annoying, 'the party you're calling is unavailable' message."

"You sure you dialed the right number? Seems to me in this day and age you should be able to reach anyone—anywhere."

"Yeah," he said, tucking his hands into his jeans' pockets. "I thought so, too. Guess I'll just have to keep trying."

"You're welcome to use the phone inside—that is, if you think the problem might be with your cell."

"Thanks, but I'm sure I'll get him next time. It's probably nothing more than a case of him forgetting to charge his battery. I'll get hold of him through one of the guys in his party."

"Oh." Had Jake been lying about enjoying her company, because at the moment, he couldn't seem to get away fast enough. "Okay, then, I guess you'd better get going. Have a safe trip."

"You, too," he said, already halfway down the front porch steps. "And send me a picture of you riding one of those llamas."

"Sure. Will do."

Candy stood there watching him, slowly twirling locks of her hair, wishing she had a logical reason for the questions clouding her mind. Questions such as, Why hadn't he at least hugged her goodbye? Should she have asked him to stay? And why would she have wanted either of those things?

Perhaps most disturbing of all…if Jake did get in touch with his pilot, and he and Bonnie did fly home tomorrow, what happened then?

Did his precious pink bundle get carted off to live with stuffy old Elizabeth Mannford?

The thought struck terror in Candy's soul.

For while she could never be Bonnie's mother, she certainly wanted Jake to be Bonnie's father. Clearly the baby adored him, just as Jake adored her.

Problem was, without breaking her personal vow to never again become a wife—let alone a mother—what could Candy do to ensure that Bonnie and Jake were never split apart?

Hot tears slid down her cheeks only to be whisked away by a chilly lake breeze. She wiped at them anyway, glad for the activity that if only for a second took her mind off the decision Jake had forced her to make. Oh, sure, for the record, he said he'd withdrawn his proposal. That he'd find some other way to keep Bonnie in his life. But what other ways did he have? If the social worker told him the best way to sway a judge was by making a lasting commitment with a woman he shared history with, then as far as Candy knew, she was it for his choices.

Which only raised one more question. Why?

Jake was handsome, didn't have bad breath. Not only worked for a living, but made a darned good living. He might not have been college educated, but he'd gone to the college of hard knocks and graduated at the top of his class. He was funny, articulate, and even made a great ham sandwich. Sheesh, what more did those Palm Breeze women want?

Candy rubbed her hands across her chilled arms, gazing over the porch rail at the play of moonlight on waves.

How many times had she and Jake shared this view?

He used to mean everything to her.

Life would have been so much easier if only she could have made him understand how strongly she felt about never subjecting a child to the kind of emotional abuse her mother had committed against her.

Life would have been easier, yes, but their marriage still would have ended the same since Valerie's gene pool had seen to it that Candy would never make a good wife, either.

JAKE EASED INTO the dark motel room, careful not to wake the angel resting her cheek on his shoulder.

Lord, what a night.

Shutting the door behind him, by rote he slid the chain lock into place, then leaned hard against the cold steel. The newly refurbished room smelled of fresh carpet and paint—almost as if the very air had been sanitized for his protection. How many nights a year did he live in rooms much like this? Oh, sure, the motels might have been hotels with five stars after their name and twenty floors of breathtaking views, but essentially, they were all the same.

Lifeless. Faceless. Soulless.

Sighing, he let the parking lot light slivering past rubber-backed drapes guide him to the desk lamp. A hundred watts of yellow incandescence did nothing to soften his view. Unless, of course, he happened to be gazing at Bonnie.

He loved her more than he'd ever thought it was possible to love another human being. He'd once loved Candy to that degree, but when it had become painfully clear that she didn't return his love, he forced himself to disconnect his.

With Bonnie, though, there was no question of her loving him. It was a gift she gave freely without a clue as to the turmoil his failing to marry Candy might bring to her tiny life.

Tugging off her pink cap, he settled Bonnie into the motel-provided crib before slipping off her baby sneakers. Undoubtedly exhausted from her hard night of play with Warren and Franny's kids, her only movement was to roll onto her side with a wet sigh.

Jake's neck, shoulder and chest still held her warmth, and in that instant he realized no matter what the personal cost, he'd do anything to keep this child in his life. Somewhere along the line, his feelings for her had passed rational to enter the realm of being ready, willing and able to lay down his life for her. Somewhere along the line, he'd become a real parent, and all at once, that knowledge was exhilarating yet terrifying. For this was the one field in which he must never fail.

Pressing hard at his temples, he willed himself to think.

How do I get Candy to marry me? And if she won't, how do I explain to a six-month-old that my love wasn't strong enough to keep her?

Releasing a confused sigh laced with exhaustion, he turned to the minifridge and pulled out a cola. He'd rather have had a beer, but in his Super Parent mode, chose to abstain.

He popped the top and took a long swig.

Sat down hard on the edge of the bed.

On a purely relationship level, the night had been a success.

Unfortunately, where his relationship stood with Candy didn't mean a hill of beans unless she was willing to take their newfound friendship and convert it back into marriage—which she might have been, if only he hadn't taken Warren up on his ridiculous reverse-psychology theory.

The scheme had looked good on paper, but Jake was from the old school of thoughts on women, meaning in his experience, honesty was generally the best policy.

But seeing how he was already too deep into Warren's plan to come clean with Candy, that left him with only two options.

Option A: dig himself an even deeper hole by claiming he still hadn't been able to reach his pilot.

Or Option B: make good on his word and actually go home.

Obviously, Option B was out of the question, which meant first thing in the morning, Candy would be having two guests for breakfast.

KELLY SNATCHED THE LAST of the half dozen glazed donuts she'd brought by. After swallowing a bite she said, "Why don't you just ask Jake to stay?"

"Because he was the one who suggested he go." Still toying with her first donut, Candy added, "I mean, if he wants to go, who am I to ask him to stay?"

"Who *are* you?" Kelly choked on a swig of coffee. "You're the only woman on this planet who can assure him of gaining custody of his baby. Don't you get it? You hold all his cards, Candy. Without you, he's screwed. Toast. Up a creek with a broken paddle. Stuck in the water without a raft. Drowning without—"

"Okay, okay, I get it!" All that mention of water made Candy's head swim. "Sheesh, I asked you over to help me work through this headache—not make it worse. Anyway, all the theorizing in the world won't help when he's probably already on his way back to Florida."

Kelly licked glaze from her fingers. "You don't know that for sure."

"Practically for sure. He said he was leaving first thing this morning."

"So? Call him anyway. That way, at least you'll know one way or the other."

"But, Kelly, I—"

"Grr!" Kelly jumped to her feet and marched to the hall table phone. "Good grief, must I do everything for you?"

Candy leaped to her feet, as well, sprinting to the phone. "Don't you dare call. I said I'd do it, so let me."

Still holding tight to the phone, Kelly said, "I'll do it!"

"He's my husband. I'll do it!"

"He's your *ex*-husband, and I'll do it!"

An ear-splitting whistle filled the room.

Both women froze then turned in unison to look toward the now open screen door.

There stood Jake, Bonnie in his arms, grinning as if she thought Candy and Kelly were the funniest thing since flung peas and carrots.

"Morning, ladies," Jake said, freshly shaven, dressed in full business regalia of black suit, cobalt shirt and matching tie, hair still adorably mussed, sexy grin in place, and what had to be the world's most adorable baby resting her head on his right shoulder. Just as Candy knew she'd be lucky to find her next breath, she knew she'd never seen her ex look more handsome.

"Morning, Jake," Kelly said, grinning as if only seconds earlier she and Candy had been calmly discussing the weather. "What brings you by?"

"I had some time before my plane gets here, so I thought I'd stop in for one more quick chat." As if he owned the place, he sauntered to the sofa, propped

Bonnie into a corner with pillows, then eased down beside her.

"Chat about what?" Candy asked.

Kelly elbowed her hard in the ribs, mumbling under her breath, "Ask him to stay."

"No," Candy whispered back. "He's obviously ready to go."

"Are you dense? He obviously wants to stay, or he wouldn't have stopped by on his way to the airport."

"You don't know that."

"Yes, I do."

"Don't."

"Do!" Candy shouted, so deep into their argument that she forgot they had an audience.

Bonnie burst into a wail.

"Now you did it," Kelly said. Rolling her eyes, she said to Jake, "When it comes to kids, your ex is the world's biggest klutz."

"I am not," Candy said, crossing to the sofa where she scooped the baby into her arms. "Bonnie likes me, don't you, sweetie?" She made a few kissy noises, tickling the infant's belly and the underside of her chin. "Come on, Bonnie, show me your pretty smile. I'm sorry mean old Kelly made you cry."

"Me? Mean?" Kelly made a beeline for the baby, too. "Don't you listen to cranky old Aunt Candy," she cooed to the still-teary-eyed-but-grinning infant. "She might have a sweet sounding name, but inside she's as crunchy as a box of icky old rocks."

By this time Bonnie was full-out laughing and Candy raised the hem of her long T-shirt to dry the corners of the child's fathomless blue eyes. "There you go," Candy said. "That's much better. A girl as pretty as you should never, ever cry."

Kelly interjected, "Unless Amanda Perkins steals your new boyfriend. Then you can cry all you want—at least until you plot how to best get even."

Rolling her eyes Candy said, "Don't you listen to a word Auntie Kelly says. Nice girls never get even, they just date men ten times more handsome and rich."

"Ooooh, I like that," Kelly said. "R-i-c-h. The classy way to spell revenge."

Jake, stepping up behind them, cleared his throat. "I hate to spoil this all-girl gabfest but, Kelly, if you don't mind, I really do need to talk to Candy before I go."

"Oh, sure," Kelly said. "Go right ahead. Because, actually, she needs to talk to you, too."

Candy gave her supposed friend another elbow to her ribs.

"Oh, yeah? What about?" Jake took squirming Bonnie from Candy's arms.

"She was wondering if maybe you could stay a couple more days."

"Kelly, I—"

"Sorry, ladies, but I really can't. My secretary scheduled me in meetings up to my kazoo, plus I set up a few appointments with potential mommies I used to date."

While the news that she wasn't Jake's only option for keeping Bonnie should have been music to her ears, the note it struck in Candy's heart sounded more like chaos. If that was the way Jake wanted it—fine.

She wanted him to go.

She wanted to pack for her trip to Peru, and to spend a leisurely week working at Candy Kisses and saying goodbye to friends. The last thing she wanted was to be distracted by Jake and his adorable baby.

Right. If all of that was true, why did the mere thought of Jake and his pink bundle heading back to Florida fill her mind, heart and soul with dread?

Nibbling her lower lip she said, ''You know, now that Kelly mentioned it, it really would be a shame for you to leave before the reunion. I mean, I hate for you to miss seeing your old friends just because of some silly argument we had.''

Candy's heart gave a funny lurch when Jake kissed Bonnie on top of her head before leveling his gaze with hers. ''Your arguments weren't silly, Candy. They made a lot of sense.''

''I know. I'm just saying that if you were to stay for the week, maybe I—''

''What, Candy? Because if you're suggesting maybe you'll feel differently about marrying me, I doubt it. In fact, I wouldn't even want you to. I'd feel guilty—like I pressured you into something you didn't want to do.''

Kelly blurted, ''Shouldn't Candy make that decision for herself?''

''Butt out,'' Candy and Jake said in unison while still staring at each other.

Candy licked her lips. ''Really, Jake, if you'd like to stay—just for the reunion. I'd love to have you.''

"You mean, you want me to rearrange my schedule to stay here? At your house?" While a slow grin parted Jake's lips, his eyebrows raised.

"Yes!" Kelly said.

"No!" Candy said. "I meant, here, as in town."

"Oh." His grin and eyebrows fell.

"Bummer," Kelly said. "We could have invited a guy over for me and had a big slumber party."

"Shouldn't you be at work?" Candy asked.

"I suppose so, but watching the two of you is a whole lot more interesting than doing Bankcroft, Stanley and Yiilosovetch's books."

Jake said, "How about if I pay you to go?"

"Seriously?"

When he reached for his wallet Candy said, "Kelly, you wouldn't *really* take his money?"

He flashed a twenty. "This do?"

"Absolutely. 'Bye." Just like that, she breezed out the front door. Just as badly as Candy had wanted her to leave, she now wished her friend had stayed.

In her most grown-up voice, Candy said to the most childish man she knew, "I can't believe you did that."

"What? Money talks. Lucky for us, Kelly was in the mood to listen."

Candy wanted to stay mad at him, truly she did, but with him once again wielding that sexy grin, unbuttoning the top button of his shirt and loosening his tie, he looked more like the incorrigible teen she'd fallen in love with than the man she'd taught herself to hate.

But then hate was a pretty strong word. She'd never really *hated* Jake, had she?

More like strongly disliked, and even that was mostly because they'd so bitterly disagreed on the subject of having kids—not because he'd snored or kicked stray dogs or was mean to old people.

To the contrary, Jake, as a husband, had been just about perfect, except for his habit of leaving dirty clothes on the floor and dirty dishes in every room of the house but the kitchen. Oh—and then there was his tendency to overspend at the grocery store, but now that he had tons of money and his very own kitchen, she supposed that was no longer an issue.

So what was the issue?

Twirling her hair while nibbling her lower lip, Candy snuck a peek at her ex.

He'd removed his tie and unfastened the next two shirt buttons in line. Lying Bonnie on the sofa, he tickled the tip of her nose with the end of said tie before tossing his suit jacket to the coffee table.

Oh, well, at least it wasn't on the floor.

"Uh, Jake?" she asked.

"Yeah?" He didn't look up from playing with the baby.

"Did you make a decision on what you're going to do? Because whatever you do, I have to get over to Candy Kisses. I have lots and lots of Coco Locos to make." *Not mention lots and lots of reasons to escape you!*

"Well, yeah, I made a decision," he said, finally glancing up. "I thought I was canceling my appointments and staying here."

"Yes, here in town, but not at our—I mean, *my* house, right?"

"You sure?"

"About what?" He'd tucked Bonnie into a safe nest of sofa pillows and now stood entirely too close. All at once he was brandishing that grin and his aftershave—not to mention a considerable amount of dangerously raw sex appeal. At this point, she wasn't even sure of her own name.

"You know. Me staying here."

"Right," she said, licking her lips and taking a healthy step back. "Yes, that's perfectly okay with me."

"Great. I'll go get our stuff, and then we can all head down to Candy Kisses to help with those Coco Locos."

"Wait," Candy called. "What exactly is it you think I just agreed to?"

"Me and Bonnie staying here at the house with you. You did change your mind, didn't you? Because look how comfy she is on your sofa." Just as he gestured her way, Bonnie tipped to her side, gumming Candy's best Indian silk throw pillow. Jake lurched forward, replacing the pillow with the baby's favorite frog teething toy. "See? Like I was saying, she's much more content here than at that cold, impersonal motel. Besides, on such short notice, who knows if they even have a room available for tonight?"

Though Candy was smart enough to know good and well when she was being bamboozled, she didn't have it in her to hand Bonnie an eviction notice.

Jake—yes—she could have booted him out the

door in seconds. But Bonnie…she was another story. The poor little thing had already been through so much.

"Okay," Candy said with a sigh. "Both of you can stay. But I'm warning you, first hint I get that this is all part of an elaborate scheme to get me to change my mind about marrying you, you're outta here."

He pouted. "You'd send an innocent babe out onto the streets?"

"Bonnie could stay. As for you, Jake Peterson, there's not an innocent bone in your body."

Chapter Six

Jake had always been fond of watching other people cook fancy food, and he certainly liked eating the fruits of their labors. What he wasn't particularly fond of was partaking in the process himself. Which was why, standing at the industrial-size stove in Candy Kisses' kitchen, he felt about as graceful as a pro hockey player performing his first ice ballet.

He cleared his throat, asking Candy, "What exactly is it I'm needing to do here? Because the more I stir, the less happens."

"Sorry," Candy said, leaving her task of shredding coconut to help him. "Caramel's a tricky thing. Want to do the shredding and I'll take over here?"

"No. Hell, no. I can do this." *Assuming you take about two steps back so I'm not surrounded in—you.* Was it her sweet scent driving him wild, or did this whole place smell deliciously of her? Focusing on the brown glop in his pan instead of the perspiration glistening on her chest, the wings of her collarbone and upper lip, he all but growled, "Just tell me what's supposed to happen."

"Duh. It turns into caramel." To help him stir, she put her hand just above his on the wooden spoon. At first, he put a little too much force into the motion, splattering some of the future caramel onto her forearm and pale yellow T-shirt.

"Ouch," she shrieked, jumping back.

Straight into him.

"Oh, jeez," he said, dropping the spoon. "Oh, man, what to do?" Plunging into hero mode, he grabbed hold of her arm and brought it to his mouth to lick the scalding liquid clean. Her skin tasted sugar-coated—not just of future caramel, but of her.

Great.

Here he was trying to save her from a serious burn and all he could think of was how just being near her fanned serious flames behind his fly.

"I think I'll survive," she said, tugging on her arm.

Reluctantly he let her go. "You never can be too careful. Isn't there some rule about spitting on burns?"

"I've heard of peeing on jellyfish stings, but not licking burns."

He shrugged, once again pulling her wounded arm to his lips, kissing not just her already-fading red mark, but a blazing trail right on up to her inner elbow where he blew a wet raspberry that sent her into a shrieking fit of giggles. "Stop it, Jake!"

"Stop what, Candy?" He had fun playing the innocent, but he had an even better time watching her pupils grow and darken. *Deny it all you want, Candy Cane, but I think you feel a little something for me, too.*

"You know what. Now, here," she said, handing him the spoon. "Stir. I'll be surprised if this batch isn't already ruined."

"If it was, even you'd have to admit it was for a good cause."

"Oh? And what's that?"

"Why, your safety, of course."

"Oh, of course. And now that you've achieved that objective—stir. And keep a close eye on the thermometer. You don't want it above two-forty-eight. There you go...good. Now, before you know it, voilà—you'll have made caramel." She slid in front of him to supervise.

Jake winced when her backside brushed against his front, creating a whole new voilà behind his fly.

"Cool," he said when all his stirring finally paid off. "When do we get to eat it?"

"You don't. Remember? This batch is being made to sell."

"Damn."

From her high chair situated a safe distance from the stove, Bonnie clanged a spoon against the oak tray. "Abba blabba gigglioo!"

"Want a taste, sweetie?" Candy dipped a fresh spoon into the pan to withdraw a pint-size dollop that she blew on to cool before holding to Bonnie's mouth. "Good, huh?" she asked when the grinning infant licked and sucked. Turning to Jake, Candy said, "I don't know much about babies, but I'd say this one already has a considerable sweet tooth."

"Why do you do that?" Jake asked.

"Do what?"

"Put yourself down when it comes to your skills with kids? Because from what I've seen of you around Bonnie, you're a natural."

He saw her swallow hard, and in that instant the mood transformed from a team spirit of accomplishment to annoyance and distrust.

Lips pressed tight, hands fisted on her hips, Candy said, "Your staying in town is just a setup, isn't it? Every move you've made has been calculated to play with my emotions."

"Come on, Candy. You should know from my practically booed-off-the-stage performance in our senior musical that I'm a rotten actor. You're giving me way too much credit and not keeping enough for yourself. Face it, whether you want to believe me, or not, Bonnie likes you. And I think you're starting to like her, too."

Arms crossed, Candy said, "Of course, I like her, Jake. She's a baby. Only jealous siblings don't *like* babies. It's just that I…I don't know. I don't know what to do with myself around them. They're like little aliens, you know? Creatures sent here from another world just to confuse and torture us earthlings." She managed to crack a small smile.

"Torture? Pretty strong choice in words, don't you think?"

"What I think, is that we should change the subject." She turned her back on him but, hands on her shoulders, he turned her right back around.

"I think you're afraid."

"Of what?"

"Of the way Bonnie makes you feel."

''That's crazy.''

''Is it, Candy?'' Was he only imagining things, or could he see the pulse pounding at the base of her throat? ''You know,'' he said, softening his tone, trying to sound less confrontational. ''Since you know you're no longer my sole option for a temporary wife, you might as well open up. Tell me why for all those years you were so dead set against being a mom to my children.''

As she leaned hard against the counter, a tremor shuddered through her. ''Don't do this, Jake. It's not the time or place.''

''When would be the right time? And there's never been a more perfect place. This is home to you, Candy, which means you've got home field advantage. Hell, I'm just trying to figure out what went wrong. Help me,'' he said, slipping his fingers beneath her chin to drag her gaze to his. ''Help me understand what makes you tick—or rather, not tick where you and the topic of kids is concerned.''

''It's not as if you don't know.''

''Oh, you mean about your mom?''

''Yes, about my mom. This is what I'm talking about. Where she's concerned, I've never told you before about my fears because I thought you'd see them as being about as realistic as Bigfoot stomping through the kitchen door. But in my heart, where it counts, I know the legacy she left me is real.

''She was a horrible mother, Jake. Leaving me alone for hours on end. Telling my father I was with a sitter, when in reality, the only thing sitting with me was the TV and my Barbie dolls. I'd be so afraid, but never say a word, because I didn't want to get her into trouble with Daddy. Most of all, I didn't want her mad at me—not because she'd yell, but because she wouldn't. Her form of punishment was this cold shoulder I could never get past. Don't you see, Jake?''

Eyes welling, she pressed her hands to her chest. ''That's who I am inside. That's all she left me, was the memory of how a mom isn't supposed to behave.''

''That's bull. You don't really believe you'll just one day turn into her, do you?''

''Yes.'' The almost crazed fear in her tear-filled eyes told him she did. After all these years, Valerie Jacobs still had hold of her daughter, the sweetest, most-deserving-of-love woman to this day Jake had ever encountered. ''Even you have to admit that toward the end of our marriage, I'd become the mirror image of her—you said so yourself with that crack about how just like my mother I was cheating on my husband—only I used Candy Kisses as a substitute lover.''

''Jeez, woman.'' Raking his fingers through his hair, Jake released a deep sigh. ''That was like… what? Over ten years ago? I said that in a moment of anger. I didn't really mean it. I was— Hell, I don't know what I was. Upset. Jealous. Admittedly, a whole lot afraid I was on the verge of losing my best friend, lover and wife. And lo and behold, look what happened. The very thing I was most afraid of came true.''

He'd unintentionally raised his voice and Bonnie had started to cry. Automatically he went to her, but

Candy had beaten him to the high chair and already held Bonnie in her arms, making soft shushing sounds that melted his heart.

"This needs to stop," Candy said. "Maybe we'd be better off just leaving the past in the past, because I can see this conversation is headed the same way all of our others on this very topic used to go."

"Where's that?"

"Straight into the toilet. Speaking of which..." Candy patted Bonnie's rump. "Looks like somebody left a little surprise for her daddy."

Jake wrinkled his nose. "Why me? You're the one holding her."

"I don't know how to change a diaper, remember?"

He grinned. "Yeah, well, maybe it's high time you learned."

TEN MINUTES LATER, a freshly diapered baby between them at one of the tables in the shop's loft, Candy scooped up a spoonful of warm blackberry cobbler and ice cream to give Bonnie a taste.

The baby grinned, gumming at the sweet purple sauce. In seconds, her normally cherry-colored lips were stained purple. But far from being upset over Bonnie's getting dirty, Candy thought the mess made her all the more adorable.

"It was pretty brilliant of you to open the second story into a loft," Jake said, spoon to his lips as he gazed around the airy space. "I see why folks like eating here—I mean, aside from your cooking. The cobbler is delicious, by the way."

"Thank you," she said, warmed by his praise. After their war of words, she'd expected to still feel bitter toward him—at the very least, sullen and withdrawn. But if anything, she felt surprisingly free, as if in admitting just how strongly she felt about her mother's legacy she'd unburdened herself of a heavy emotional weight.

Sure, he might think she was crazy, but she didn't care. At least now he knew where she stood on the subject of having kids, which meant the issue of their remarrying was well and truly behind them and they could get on with the business of renewing their friendship. Which, truth be told, she'd missed over the years worse than any other aspect of their marriage.

She missed consulting with him about paint chips for the house and about what they should have for dinner and which laundry detergent he thought was the best buy.

It might sound corny, but while she'd failed miserably at being a wife, she'd always considered herself a good friend. And once upon a time, Jake had been not just a friend, but her very best friend.

If only for that reason alone, I owe it to Jake to pretend to be his wife. Bonnie's mother.

The thought hit hard from out of nowhere, turning Candy's stomach into a swirl of confusion.

She didn't owe Jake anything. Or did she?

He said, "You turned quiet. Something else you wanted off your chest?"

"Besides this caramel stain?"

"If you want," he said with a brash wink. "I know a trick that'll get that stain right out."

"I'll just bet," she said, giving the cooing baby another bite of cobbler.

"Seriously, I do. But first, you'll have to take it off." He didn't even have the decency to redden.

Candy couldn't help but laugh. The last time she'd fallen for this trick she'd been twenty-two, and not only had Jake conned her into removing her shirt, but all of her other clothes, as well!

"That's not a touch of pink flaming your cheeks, is it?"

"No!" *Yes!*

"You wouldn't be thinking about that night we did it on top of the washer, would you?"

"*Jake!*" Even though she knew full well they were alone in the shop, out of habit, Candy looked around to see if anyone might have heard. "I can't believe you just said that in front of the baby."

"Why? It's not like she understood."

"I don't care. It's the principle of the thing."

"Fine. You tell me you remember, and I'll drop the whole topic. I'll even change the subject to something nice and safe—like your favorite candy recipe."

"I'll tell you no such thing."

"Why? Afraid I'll sell your secret to some international corporate spy who goes by the name of Sven?"

"No, I'm not afraid of anything. I just don't feel like discussing our…well, you know what."

"Say it, Candy."

"Say what?"

He grabbed hold of her left hand, ran his thumb along the inside of her palm. "Come on, I wanna hear you say *sex life*."

"Why?"

"Because just saying the word sex always used to make you blush. Just for old time's sake, I wanna see if it still does."

A dizzying heat flamed her cheeks from just thinking about the word, let alone the act! "You've been spending entirely too much time in the bug spray aisles of your stores."

"How can you tell?"

"Have you been listening to yourself? You've gone plum crazy."

"Over you."

Where they had been playing, Candy's next comment was dead serious. "Please, Jake, don't say something like that when you don't mean it."

"Who says I didn't? These past couple days with you have been tight. I don't know what's going on. Hell, the last thing I ever expected was, well…" Breaking the lock he'd had on her gaze, he released a deep sigh. "I guess this custody thing with Bonnie has me all screwed up. I mean, I've always thought you were hot, but seeing you now, it's like all of the sudden you're *super* hot."

While Bonnie contentedly gummed her spoon, Jake laced his long, strong fingers with Candy's. "Come on, don't leave me hanging. Please, tell me you're feeling whatever this is, too."

"I…I don't know what I'm feeling," she said, mind and heart reeling from his admission. Not that he'd said all that much, but reading between the lines had given her a pretty fair idea of where his thoughts had been headed.

"I'll admit, I have at times since you've been here realized how much I've missed you. But that doesn't erase what happened, Jake. Just because we might still have physical sparks between us, that doesn't mean our goals are any closer to lining up. Hear me on this, and hear me well—I will never marry again, and I certainly will never have kids. You, on the other hand, already have a beautiful baby girl. That pretty much sums up where our relationship—or what's left of it—can go. No matter how good we might feel together, the bottom line is that there never really was, and will certainly never be, a *we*."

"DAMN, JAKE, my hat's off to ya, buddy." Dietz shook his head, gazing wide-eyed at Jake as if his old friend had climbed to hero status. Warren and Rick were in the break room, too, scarfing down heaping servings of Franny's homemade macaroni and cheese. Bonnie was "helping" a couple high school girls stock swim toys. "I always knew you had a special way with the ladies, but man, oh, man did you put Warren's plan to work. I thought for sure Candy would have kicked your butt out of town by now."

"Whoa, slow down there," Rick said. "Golden Boy here didn't do all *that* good. He might still be in town. Heck, he even wormed his way into staying at Candy's house, but the harsh reality is that she can't stand him any more now than the day he last left town."

"Thanks, Rick." Arms crossed, nerve ticking in his jaw, Jake glared his supposed buddy's way. "With friends like you, who needs enemies?"

"My pleasure, man. Any time."

Jake rested his elbows on the break room table, fisting the hair at his temples. "I don't know, guys. I thought I had this thing figured out, but somewhere along the line what I thought was just a game I was playing to keep Bonnie got personal. What if Candy gets hurt?"

What if I get hurt by falling for her all over again?

The mere thought—no matter how unlikely—landed Jake in a cold sweat.

"You thought no one would get hurt?" Warren asked. "We're talking about you holding on to your kid here. Them's some incredibly high stakes. If some distant relative flounced in here trying to take one of my kids, there's no telling what I'd do. Suffice to say, I wouldn't give either of them up without one helluva fight."

"Yeah, but that's just it. This is my fight. Not Candy's. What right do I have to bring her into this?"

Warren shrugged.

Dietz studiously chewed on the end of a straw.

Rick studied the Avon catalog that Mona from women's golf had left on the table.

Frowning, Jake said, "So all of you think I was wrong to ask Candy to remarry me?"

"Not exactly wrong," Warren pointed out. "Just not exactly right—though your proposal was logical from anyone's perspective. What else could you do?"

"Damn straight," Dietz said around his straw.

Rick turned to the lipstick section. "Wow, did you all have any idea how much gunk women slide around on their lips?"

Jake sighed.

He didn't at all like the turn his Find Bonnie A Mommy project had taken. Sure, he was still in town, but to what end?

Candy seemed pretty focused on the fact that she wasn't marrying or having kids, so where did that leave him? Would he be better off back in Palm Breeze preparing for legal battle with Elizabeth Mannford rather than trying to transform himself into some judge's model image of the ideal family man?

No.

Mrs. Starling herself admitted that taking the single-dad legal route could take years.

If only he could get Candy to come 'round to his way of thinking, they could be married by the end of the week. Bonnie could be his by the end of the month, because surely Elizabeth Mannford was smart enough to bow out gracefully once she realized she didn't stand a snowball's chance of taking Bonnie from him *and* his wife.

No. He'd come too far to give up just yet. And now, with him and Bonnie camping in enemy territory, not only would it be easier to call a truce, but to work out an equitable marriage agreement beneficial for everyone. All he had to do was to show Candy a glimpse of the great year the three of them could have. And then all she'd have to do is say yes!

Sounded doable, but he needed a little something extra. Something to really cinch the deal.

"So, Jake," Warren asked. "Need any help movin' into Candy's place?"

"Nah. Me and Bonnie don't have much stuff."

"Too bad," Rick said, looking up from his catalog. "I was watching one of those court shows the other day and this landlord and ex-renter were fightin' over this really sharp sofa and chairs the renter left in the apartment."

"Does this story have a point?" Dietz asked.

"High-five, man," Jake said, raising his hand to Dietz's. "I was just wondering the same thing."

"Shoot, yeah, this has a point," Rick said, puppy-dog-brown eyes looking wounded. "The judge ruled in favor of the landlord—not just because the renter owed like six months of back rent, but because of some goofy possession is nine-tenths of the law thing…or maybe it was eight-sixths? Anyway—"

"Rick, my man, you and that judge are freakin' geniuses." Suddenly the answer to Jake's dilemma was staring him right in the face. He wouldn't just move in to his old house, but he'd move in lock, stock and barrel. He was talking great furniture. State-of-the-art entertainment system. And most important—a fully stocked nursery complete with wind-up toys, mobiles and a super-cute baby.

He and Bonnie would be so firmly entrenched in Candy's house that even she couldn't boot them out. Not only that, but being around his great taste in furniture and expensive toys, would give his ex a first-hand look at how much fun they'd have living in his plush Palm Breeze digs.

Perfect. His plan was absolutely, positively perfect.

Now all he had to do was put it into action. "Hey, guys," he said. "Anyone up for some serious shopping?"

"WHAT'S ALL THIS?" Candy shrieked upon walking through her front door. She would have calmly asked the question, but a sci-fi space flick was blaring too loud for anything but a howling extraterrestrial to be heard above the roar.

Where her old but comfy chintz sofa and wing chairs used to live, now sat a hulking black-leather sectional with built-in recliners on both ends.

Sleeping Jake, Bonnie snoozing in his arms, lounged in the one with the best view of the TV.

Speaking of which, her mini-TV had been replaced by the Mt. Everest of big screens, accompanied by enough woofers and tweeters to shake down an entire galaxy!

Candy struggled to hold tight to her fury. Really, she did. But one look at Jake and his pink-cheeked daughter replaced her rage with melancholy.

Swallowing hard, she remembered happier times when both her grandfather and Jake had fallen asleep in front of John Wayne World War II movies and Westerns. And how, if the room was a little nippy, she'd cover them both with one of the many antique afghans her grandmother had crocheted.

Creeping to the series of black-and-gray remotes on the coffee table, she spent a moment studying them, then switched everything off.

Bonnie wailed.

Jake lurched upright. "What the—"

"Sorry," Candy said, startled herself. "I thought quiet would help you two nap more soundly, not wake up."

Turning Bonnie toward him, he cuddled her to his chest, kissing the top of her head. "Shh, it's okay. Mean old Auntie Candy didn't mean to wake you up."

"Hey, *mean old Auntie Candy* was trying to do you and your munchkin a favor, mister." Hands on her hips, she said, "Although now that you're up, mind explaining where all of this came from and when it's going back?"

He pretended to look innocent. "Amazing. I was just dreaming about all this and then—poof. I guess while I was sleeping, the Afternoon Nap Fairy must have dropped by."

"Afternoon Nap Fairy my behind."

"Hey, watch it," he said, covering Bonnie's ears. "There's a child present."

"Yeah, *you.*"

"Oh," he said, clutching his chest. "That hurts, Candy Cane. And since when is it a crime to buy a beautiful woman a small housewarming gift even if you are leaving town?"

"A cookbook or flowers would have been appropriate. What you've done is more like moving in. Besides which, this mammoth beast you think is a sofa doesn't even match the house."

"Fine, I'll have something else here within the hour, just pleeeeease." Holding tight to Bonnie, he slid off the chair and to his knees. Fingertips steepled, he said, "Pleeease don't make me take back the TV. She told me she likes it here."

"Oh, *she* did, did she?"

He nodded, hobbling on his knees to her side of the room. Upon reaching her, he curled his fingers into the hip pocket of her jeans to help pull himself up.

Candy's Jake and Bonnie proximity alarms wailed out of control—especially when even after Jake was standing, he kept his right hand snuggly in her pocket.

Voice teasingly low, he added, "Don't tell anyone, but her name is Lola. She used to be a showgirl, but a bum ankle forced her out of the limelight and into our living room." Humming a crushingly familiar tune, Jake danced Bonnie's bare feet across Candy's chest, thrilling her with a whole kind of light—lights made of twinkling awareness for this man and his baby that shimmered through her body with the excitement of a thousand tiny fireworks.

"Oh," Candy said, licking her lips before shuffling back. That old Barry Manilow song, "Copacabana," had been big the summer she was in fourth grade, or had it been third? She couldn't remember, probably because the only thing about that summer she could remember was her newfound fascination with Jake.

That had been the summer his family moved to Lonesome from Springdale, Arkansas. Jake's maternal grandmother lived in town, and they'd relocated to Lonesome to care for her.

Before encountering Jake at the city pool wearing jean cutoffs and a cool Scooby-Doo T-shirt, Candy had never even thought about boys, but there he'd been in all of his almost-muscled splendor. He was by far the best cannonball diver, best basket shooter, fort builder and ice-cream truck chaser she'd ever met. And one day, she'd promised herself, he would be hers. They'd get married and raise a dozen kids and even buy both a box turtle and an iguana for pets. Maybe if they were really lucky, they'd even live in a Winnebago and park it down by the river.

Still swaying Bonnie's chubby legs to an imaginary beat, Jake said, "Remember how many ice-cream sandwiches we ate that summer while my sister played that record over and over and—"

She put her hands to his lips. "I remember."

"Then why so glum? Those were good times."

Yes, they were—at least when she was with him and the rest of the gang of misfits they'd had the run of town with. Warren, Kelly, Dietz. Becky moved in the sixth grade. Rick didn't move into town until the seventh grade, by which time, Kelly and Candy had been banished from the group. No females allowed.

When she'd been with her friends, Candy forgot about what waited for her once she got home. True, once she'd started living with her grandfather, life had gotten much better, but she'd never been able to completely forget what had gone on before her mother had left and her father died.

"You're not thinking about your mom again, are you?"

Candy nodded.

"Why do you give her ghost this much power?"

"How do you know she's dead?"

"How do you know she's not?"

She shrugged.

"Do you want to know? If you do, I could hire a P.I. and we'd be onto to her just like that." When he snapped his fingers, Bonnie grinned, trying to capture his right hand.

"No. The last thing I want to do is to find her." Candy sighed then took a seat on the black beast that impersonated a sofa. Leaning back, it gripped her like a skilled lover. "My gosh, is this comfortable."

"Shoot, yeah," Jake said, landing beside her. "Think I'd watch Lola from just any old couch?"

Just seeing his grin blotted out Candy's dark memories and ushered in warm sun—sun that bore more and more resemblance to Jake.

Cupping Bonnie's tiny feet in her left hand, she gave them a gentle squeeze. At this moment, more than anything she could ever remember wanting in recent months, she longed to release both past and future fears to wholly embrace the present.

Meeting Jake's winsome grin with one of her own, she said, "Anyone ever tell you you're a nut?"

"All the time, Candy Cane. All the time."

THAT EVENING, while Candy was sudsing her full breasts, slim waist, kissable little belly button and all-too-grabbable backside in the shower, Jake found himself in need of a distraction from steamy memories of how much fun they used to have sharing the shower!

Why she hadn't invited him in, he had no idea, but seeing as how Bonnie was also ignoring him, happily gumming her toes, he figured he might as well find a constructive use for his few minutes alone—and fortunately, he knew just the ticket.

In the kitchen he found a list of phone numbers beside the phone. The list was old—including numbers for not only Candy's grandparents, but his parents. Swallowing hard, Jake figured the foursome would approve of what he was about to do.

Punching the number before he could change his mind, Kelly answered on the second ring. "Landon?"

Landon? Wasn't that Dietz's first name? Not that anyone ever used it. "Ah, sorry Kel, it's me—Jake."

"Oh, uh—hi, Jake. What's up?"

"Got a quick question for you."

"Okay, shoot."

"This is going to sound nuts, but by any chance do you remember Candy's mom's maiden name?"

For a few seconds the only sound on the line was theme music to *Wheel of Fortune,* then, "You know, strangely enough, I do. Claymore. Yeah, it was definitely Claymore because I remember fat Loopy Jones from two houses down used to tease her about how much makeup she wore. You know behind her back saying stuff like, 'Hey, why doncha put on more clay.'"

"Nice," Jake said.

"Yeah, last I heard Loopy was in an Oklahoma prison."

"What for?"

"Would you believe it? Armed robbery of a donut shop."

Grimacing, Jake said, "Yeah, knowing Loopy, I

believe it.'' The shower went off. Time to go. ''Anyway, Kel, thanks. That's all I needed to know.''

''Why?''

''I thought I might get a reunion together between Candy and her mom.''

''You're joking, right?''

''Uh, no.''

''Don't do it, Jake. *Please,* don't do it. Candy would be mortified—not to mention thoroughly ticked off.''

Gazing toward the ceiling, Jake closed his eyes. Mmm, just a few feet above him, Candy was sliding a fluffy white towel up and down those gorgeous thighs...

''Jake? Did you hear me?''

Attention back to the phone, he said, ''Yes, I heard you, but I still think it's a great idea.''

''One you're going to forget ever coming up with, right?'' When he didn't answer, she pressed again. *''Right?''*

Lips tight, he sighed. ''Right.''

Jake uncrossed his fingers, not even a smidgeon sorry for having told Kelly that lie. Hmm, guess she wasn't as good a friend to Candy as she claimed to be. For if she had been a true friend, she would have seen that his plan to reunite Candy with her mother made perfect sense. Once Candy saw for herself just how little she resembled the woman—not only in looks—but spirit, she'd see how ridiculous all her vows were to never be a wife or mom and immediately agree to marry him.

Immediately after that, he'd present his new bride

to Mrs. Starling and voilà—Bonnie would forever be his.

Grinning at how perfectly all of this was coming together, Jake headed upstairs to see if Candy needed help with her towel!

Chapter Seven

"Be careful, Jake! She's slippery!" From the edge of the tub, Candy struggled to keep hold of Bonnie, aka the Blue-Eyed Eel, as she swooshed and sloshed across the bottom of the tub.

"You think I don't already know that?" Jake said, calmly sliding the giggling water rat into her purple plastic tub chair.

"How should I know? Hand me the shampoo. You didn't get enough on her."

Hmm, the way Jake saw it, this just kept getting better. Candy, the self-proclaimed bumbler on all things baby looked to be doing a bang-up job. Which left his mind free to mosey on over to other topics, namely, how all that steamy bath vapor caused strands of Candy's high ponytail to escape, spiraling down the nape of her glistening neck.

If she were still his wife, it would have been no big deal for him to lean low enough to curve his mouth around that arch where her neck met shoulder. Shoot, he'd view it as his civic duty to introduce the two parts of her body, and while he was at it, he could kiss his way over to her sweat-slick chest. Then, when he licked the hollow between her breasts, she'd taste all salty and maybe even a little sweet, like the chocolates she'd made earlier that day. Lord, he wanted to taste her, smell her, make love to her till sleep claimed them both from sheer exhaustion.

Frowning, Jake wondered if the fly of his favorite jeans had always been this uncomfortable, or was a certain part of him just perpetually hard around a certain woman?

"Could you please hand me that rinse cup?" Candy asked.

"Sure," Jake said, happy for the distraction. Impressed with her zero-eye-runoff rinse technique, he asked, "Where'd you learn to do that?"

She shrugged. "Probably just seen it done in a movie sometime."

"Yeah, right. Rinsing of that caliber takes on-the-job training, sweetheart. Cough it up. On whose kid did you pick up those skills?"

She made a face at him before scrubbing Bonnie all over with a pink bath mitt.

"I'm waaaaiting…" Jake sang out.

"I'm ignoooooring…" she sang right back.

Minutes later, with Bonnie snuggly wrapped in a terry-cloth robe, bunny-eared hood locked and in the upright position, the trio tromped down the upstairs hall to the sunshine-yellow room Jake always thought would make a great nursery. Hence the reason why, along with having the sofa and TV delivered, he'd had a mahogany canopy crib, matching changing table and dresser delivered, as well. The only thing missing besides a few pictures and a thick area rug was a rocker.

No—not just any old rocker, but the one he'd painstakingly handmade for Candy to rock their future babies to sleep in. He'd been so excited about giving it to her... But from first sight she'd hated it. He'd never even seen her sit in it, let alone rock in it.

Looking back, he should have questioned her as to why. But being practically still a kid himself, he'd just swallowed his hurt feelings and chalked her dislike down to the fact that, as did most other females he'd known, she preferred gifts of jewelry to sentimental favorites.

What had she done with the old rocker? Was it in the attic gathering dust? Or had she gotten rid of it just as easily as she'd gotten rid of him? And if she had, why did the mere thought of some other woman rocking babies in his wife's rocker hurt so damned bad?

"I still can't believe while I was finishing up all those Coco Locos, you were busy buying out every furniture store in Lonesome."

Grinning like a proud little boy, he added, "I had a new oven delivered and installed, too. It has awesome space-shuttle-quality temp control and a digital timer."

"Neat," Candy said, keeping it to herself that it had been a while since she'd baked a casserole important enough to warrant aeronautical efficiency. "You were even busier than I thought. Thank you— at least for the oven."

Still beaming, he shrugged.

Candy gingerly placed Bonnie on the pink gingham changing table pad, then proceeded to do an expert lotion and diaper job.

Reminding herself that caring for Bonnie was no different from diapering the dolls she'd played with as a child, Candy forced herself to ignore all those sumptuous baby scents.

Freshly washed hair.

Freshly lotioned bottom.

She was strong. She could take it. As long as Jake didn't tag team her by throwing his own wonderful blend of scents into her already overloaded system, Candy would survive.

"Okay," Jake said, "after seeing how efficient you were with that, now I know something's up. It took me nearly a week after Bonnie was born to figure out where to put the sticky tab diaper thingees besides on my fingers. I know you didn't learn the finer points of diapering from watching a movie." Stepping behind her, he made good on her most current fears, bracing his hands on either side of her waist on the changing table rail.

Was it just her imagination, or was that really his warm breath on the back of her neck?

Focus, Candy. Keep your eyes and hands on the baby.

Don't you dare turn around and drag Jake into a kiss that'd rock the world. Well…maybe not the whole world, but at the moment, she wouldn't object to hers being a little shook up!

Argh! See? Whenever Jake hovered near her like

this, her every carefully made plan and vow flew right out the window in the face of her maddening desire to indulge in a one—or maybe even two—time wild fling!

Bonnie caught sight of him and thought he was trying to play peekaboo. Never one to disappoint his mini-miracle, he peeked around Candy's left shoulder, then booed around her right.

Bonnie's giggle rang through the still-practically-empty hardwood-floored room.

"Your daddy's silly, isn't he, Bonnie Blue?" Candy tickled the baby on her tummy, causing her to laugh even more.

"Boy, we're doing a bang-up job of getting her ready for bed, aren't we?"

"Hey," Candy said, "I thought aunties are allowed to spoil? It's real moms and dads who have to do all the dirty work, like convincing a wired baby it's an hour past her bedtime."

"*Real* moms and dads, huh?" While Bonnie gummed her right foot, Jake settled his hands loosely atop Candy's hips. The position came naturally, as if he'd been born to hold her this way. "Why do you say real, like when you become a parent, you get the keys to the real parent clubhouse?"

Not meeting his gaze, Candy said, "I don't know. I guess that's just the way I feel. Since I'll never get the chance to be a real parent, maybe I do feel that to a certain extent it's an exclusive club to which I'll never be admitted."

"That's absurd," Jake said, tucking his fingers beneath her chin, urging her gaze up to meet his. "In the past ten minutes of caring for Bonnie, you've done a better job than I still do, and I've been taking care of her off and on ever since she was born. Come on, Candy, tell me, where'd you learn all that stuff?''

"Nowhere."

"Liar, liar, pants on—"

"Baby-sitting, okay?'' Shocked by her own admission, she tore her gaze from his and moved to the other side of the room. Standing arms crossed on front of the bay window, she lost herself in the lake, in the silvery moonlight weaving a path through the waves to their house.

Jake allowed his ex a moment to herself while scooping Bonnie up and into her toy-filled crib. But then he was right back, hands loosely curved atop Candy's shoulders. "I thought you told me you've never babysat for your friends?''

"I forgot one—okay. One of the women who work for me had sitter trouble, so she brought four-month-old Lucy into work with her. Just for a little while. And maybe I might have offered to watch her once or twice after that. There. Now you know my little secret. Kelly doesn't even know. Satisfied?''

"Not hardly,'' he whispered into her ear. "What I really want to know will only come out after I probe deeper.'' Gently spinning her around, he said, "Tell me honestly, spending time with baby Lucy wasn't all that bad, was it?''

"Not after I got used to it."

"In fact, you might even say that you actually enjoyed yourself, right?''

"Well…I wouldn't go that far.''

"Bull. I think you not only liked it, I think you've been hiding a secret hankering to do it again—only this time, you want a baby of your own."

Candy's heart pounded. "That's the craziest thing I've ever heard. You know full well where I stand on the subject of having children."

"I know what you tell me, but then I also know what I see." He leaned forward to plant a lingering kiss on her cheek. "Think you can get the rug rat into her jammies for me? I've got a few business calls to make that can't be put off."

"No, I—" Too late, Jake was already whistling his way down the hall.

Alone with Bonnie, Candy fumed, not at the baby, but her insufferable father. "Is he always this big of a creep?" she asked the bubble-blowing cutie. "Pleading the fifth, huh? I'll take that as a yes."

More efficiently than she maybe would have liked, Candy dressed the baby, then scooped the bulk of stuffed animals and toys out of her crib before placing Bonnie on her back and winding the palm tree, sun and sand bucket mobile that played a tinkling version of the Beach Boys' "Surfin' U.S.A." Count on Jake to skip the whole lamb, duck and cow routine in favor of going straight for swinging-single fun on the beach.

Candy stared in wonder at Bonnie while Bonnie stared equally as hard at her.

As much as Candy hated to admit it, the kid was starting to grow on her, which could be a problem—especially now, with Bonnie and her father living under the same roof.

At least where Jake was concerned, she still carried

enough righteous indignation from their divorce to keep her cool around him—some of the time.

Okay, maybe it was now just down to occasionally keeping her cool with him, but in Bonnie's case, Candy feared she was down for the count.

Bonnie reached out to her and Candy placed her index finger in the baby's petal-soft palm, grinning when that cottony touch turned out to have an iron grip.

"You're a fighter, aren't you, sweetie?"

As if Bonnie had not only heard her, but understood, she gave a strong kick.

"What should I do? Take a chance on marrying your daddy and hope I don't fall for him all over again?"

Just putting voice to her question quickened Candy's pulse. Since when had even the thought of tying the knot all over again—even temporarily—become an option?

"And then there's you..." Candy said. "You're the real problem, because all these years I've been making my vows, I've also been keeping a secret. Wanna know what it is?"

Bonnie gave another kick.

"Okay..." Candy took a deep breath, swallowed hard. "Here it goes...now keep in mind, if you tell any of this to anyone, you're in big trouble, missy." When Candy tickled Bonnie on her tummy, the baby giggled. "Shh, now see? That's just the kind of outburst I'm talking about. If we're going to share secrets, you've got to stay quiet."

As if mirroring the emotion in Candy's heart, Bonnie stilled.

Again swallowing hard, Candy leaned further over the crib. "That's better. Now, the secret I've never told another soul is that I actually adore babies. I love everything about them from their smells to their laughs to their itty-bitty toys and jars of food. The problem is, I didn't have such a terrific mommy, and something you'll learn when you grow up is that you inherit things from your mom and dad. Some good things, some bad, but all of them are right there inside of you." Candy wiped at a few renegade tears. "So, see? Maybe I want to take Jake up on his offer a little more than I let on. Not because I like him, or anything, but because I like you."

Reaching into the crib, Candy slid her arms under the baby and lifted her, snuggling her close, her downy hair tucked beneath her chin. "I like everything about you, Bonnie Blue. Everything except for the fact that no matter how much I want to keep not just you, but dozens of other babies that are all my own, the fact of the matter is that I can never be a mom."

"You still spouting that pile of—"

"Jake!" Candy jumped. "How long have you been standing there?"

"Long enough."

"Yeah, well, you shouldn't have eavesdropped. That wasn't very nice."

"Sorry."

"No you're not."

"True. Because you just handed me some highly

potent ammunition. In fact, if a dozen years ago you had only shared with me what you just shared with Bonnie, who knows how differently our lives might have turned out?'' Crossing to her, with only Bonnie between them, he cupped his hands to her tear-damp cheeks. ''Do you realize the significance of what you've just admitted?''

Candy shook her head.

''Woman, you just said that all these years, you've secretly wanted babies—you've even expertly cared for one not only behind my back, but your best friend's.''

''So?'' Candy raised her chin.

''So, don't you see? All this time, you've claimed you couldn't be a mom because of some rotten parenting genes. But face it, Candy, in this whole wide world, there could never be a better parent than you. And you know why?''

She shook her head.

''Because you've seen the job done poorly, and in your heart, you've practiced a thousand times how to do the job right. All those times your mom let you down, your soul took notes. Her forgetting to pick you up from school, leaving you home alone when you were sick, forgetting your birthday—all of it is stored right here,'' he said, pressing his hand against her heart.

The heat of him seeped into her, warming her inside and out as effectively as hot spring sun. She wanted to believe all the pretty things he was saying, but his theory sounded too simple. Too good to be true.

Could any of it be right?

And if so, what did that imply about their marriage? Did that mean she'd been a fool to ever let Jake go? Or had it just been a case of her being right in the fact that she'd never make a good wife and wrong in the fact that she'd never make a good mom?

Argh. The confusion and pain of the whole issue hurt so bad she wanted to scream. "Here, please take her," Candy said, handing Bonnie to her dad before running from the room.

JAKE PUT BONNIE TO BED, snatched up his half of the baby monitor, then headed downstairs.

Had he pushed Candy too fast, too hard?

Maybe. But when he'd overheard her confession, he was honor-bound by his own mission to make Candy see just how unfounded her worries about ever becoming a carbon copy of her mom truly were. Back when they'd divorced over these same issues, he'd been too young, too full of pride to step back and to look objectively at the big picture. But now that Jake wasn't only older, but fresh out of pride, he didn't care what it took, as long as he didn't return to Palm Breeze without a wife.

He found Candy in the kitchen, standing at the sink, staring blankly at the dark beyond the open window, faucet running. A light breeze stirred gauzy yellow curtains along with wisps of Candy's silken hair.

Stepping behind her, he shut off the faucet. "I'm sorry if yet again I've upset you. That wasn't my intention."

"I know. Thanks for the apology."

"You're welcome."

She faced him, braced her hands against the counter behind her. "Get Bonnie all tucked in?"

"Yep."

"Good. Listen, Jake—"

"Candy, I—"

They laughed, then both said in unison, "You go first."

"No, really, you." Jake had planned on coming clean about his plan to woo her with reverse psychology, but he supposed they'd had enough turmoil for one night and his confession could wait until morning.

One thing was for sure, after seeing firsthand how angst-ridden Candy was about her issues with her mother, no matter how badly he wanted her to be his wife, she didn't deserve to be manipulated, even as innocent as he'd planned those manipulations to be. While he knew they could never again be as solid a couple as they'd been when they first married, he was at least getting the sense they could be friends. And at the moment, if he didn't have a wife, he was sure as hell going to need all the friends he could get.

"Okay," Candy said, twirling an escaped tendril from her ponytail. "I never thought I'd be saying this, but maybe all these years you've been right about my fears of becoming my mother. Maybe even spending a year with you and Bonnie could be like a trial for me, you know, with you standing by in case I suddenly flip out."

Jake's heart felt ready to burst.

Miracle of miracles, this was it, she was going to agree to marry him!

Taking her hands in his, he said, "That's not going to happen. I've already said this ten times, but I'll be happy to say it ten million more. Candy Jacobs, you're going to make an amazing mother. So? When should we tie the knot?"

"Whoa," she said, "slow down. I didn't say I would definitely marry you. I said maybe, just for a year, it'd be all right. I don't even know myself if I can do that, but I promise to have an answer for you no later than the reunion Saturday night."

"Oh." Talk about burst bubbles. Jake felt about as low as a kid who'd just lost his ticket to the circus.

"I know that's not what you want to hear," she said, squeezing his hands, "but at the moment, that's the best I can do. What I need to know from you is, for now, is that enough?"

Chapter Eight

After a restless night spent down the hall from Candy, Jake was only too happy to get up bright and early Thursday morning to make a quick trip to the store, then cook some grub.

Is that enough?

How many times had he run Candy's question through his mind? Of course, he'd told her that just having her consider his proposal meant a lot—and it did. But meaning a lot and actually agreeing with it were two vastly different things.

Hacking through a bunch of green onions for his world-famous, chili-scrambled eggs, he figured he'd done the right thing in keeping his mouth shut.

She'd already come so far in such a short time.

What he needed to do now was to lay off any talk of their future marriage in favor of showing her just how great such a venture could be—not just for Bonnie, but for them.

Satisfied with that decision, he tossed the onions into a pan of melted butter, then whipped in eggs, milk, cheese and chili. Once his "eggstravaganza" finished cooking, he popped open a can of biscuits and flung the Frisbee-shaped dough onto a cookie sheet.

Just standing in Candy's cozy kitchen filled him with memories. Did she still make from-scratch biscuits every Saturday morning?

He squeezed his eyes shut, remembering the look of her long, golden legs peeking out from under the hem of his Lonesome High football jersey. It had a few holes in conveniently strategic places and if he was real lucky, sometimes she'd still be feeling feisty enough from Friday night that she cooked without panties!

She'd bring a plate heaping with fragrant biscuits and a bowl of melted butter up to bed, where they'd lounge around wolfing down biscuits and watching cartoons. And sometimes, if butter dribbled onto her chin, he'd be forced by husbandly code of honor to personally lick that dribble clean.

Of course, then, he might have to venture lower— just to make sure none of the slick, buttery goodness had infiltrated past his jersey's neckline vee, for if it had, the shirt would have to come off.

House rule.

And once that jersey was off, and he had Candy in her full naked glory reclining like his own personal buffet across the center of the bed, could he really be blamed when the bowl of butter called out to him, urging him to dip his fingers in, then paint a buttery trail up and down and—

"Mmm, we wondered what smelled so good down here." Candy, wearing those stupid cat-print pajamas instead of his football jersey sans panties, stepped up beside him, Bonnie on her hip.

"Oh, Jake," Candy said, peering around him to peek into the pan. "Chili for breakfast? Again?"

"Hey, you just said it smelled good."

"It does, but it just doesn't seem very healthy. Wouldn't you rather have some nice cantaloupe and...I don't know? Maybe some homemade biscuits?"

"You're still making biscuits, huh?"

Her cheeks turned the color of strawberry jam. Hot damn. Looked like someone else remembered their finger-licking good games—not that he wanted to play.

Yeah, right.

"I, uh, occasionally make biscuits," she said, her free hand twirling her hair.

After sliding the frying pan off the burner, he said, "You still got my football jersey?"

Candy thought for a second about lying, but figured he'd somehow ferret out the truth, so she might as well be forthcoming right up front. "Yes, I still have it. Why? Want it back?"

He leaned against the counter, crossed his arms. "As a matter of fact, yeah. It holds a lot of fond memories for me and since you've made it clear the two of us will never again be an item, I figure I might as well give it to the next Mrs. Peterson."

Candy's throat tightened. "Whatever you say. You'll have to wait for a little while, though. I think it's dirty."

"You still wear it, huh?"

On her way to the laundry room located off the kitchen, Candy plopped the baby into her high chair, giving her a set of plastic keys to play with. "It's so old, it makes a good painting or gardening shirt."

"Oh."

She itched to turn around to see his expression so badly it hurt.

The creep.

He'd given her that jersey as a wedding present! Their wedding night, he'd said that from now on, the only moves he'd make would be for her. How dare he want it back!

Without bothering to turn on the light, Candy dug through the overflowing hamper.

Jake's showing up had put her way behind on all of her chores—not to mention the fact that all of that stupid chili and other food he kept hauling in was only putting her that much further behind in cleaning out her kitchen.

"You seem uptight," Jake said, stepping up behind her in the dark.

"Yeah, well, I'm not."

"Here, let me help."

"Don't do me any favors," Candy said between clenched teeth. For all practical purposes, that jersey was her favorite negligee—not because it reminded her of him or the things they'd done when she'd been wearing that jersey, but because, because…

That jersey represents the woman I used to be. The woman I dreamed as a little girl of becoming. It was only after she'd grown up and Jake had started in with his nagging about having kids that she'd realized that woman wasn't anyone she could ever be.

What if you were wrong?

What if all along, what Jake calls your unreasonable fears about committing your mother's same sins are just that—unreasonable. What if all along, you really had held the capability of not just being a great wife, but a great mom?

Just think what that implied.

All the joys she'd missed.

Breakfasts in bed not shared. Leisurely Saturday afternoons together spent antiquing, sailing or hiking. Shoot, for all she cared, she and her cozy family of three could do nothing more than sit around the living room staring into each other's eyes and any day would be a complete success.

Her family?

Even in the dark, Candy felt Jake—felt him as if he'd once again become a part of her she'd have a tough time letting go. But then hadn't she already been thinking along those same lines the previous night? Wasn't that why she told Jake she'd give him her answer at the reunion, because she needed more time to decide if she really was making the right decision, or if she was playing herself for a fool?

Raising her chin, she said, "You know, now that I think about it, no."

"No to what?"

"No, I won't give you back that jersey. It isn't yours, it's mine. You gave it to me fair and square and I don't feel like giving it back."

"What do you feel like?" he asked, moving in the

dark to stand entirely too close. Close enough that the heat trapped between their bodies told her he wasn't anywhere near close enough.

He'd already showered and smelled slightly damp. Clean—like soap and shampoo. And suddenly Candy, in some secret place deep inside, wasn't arguing over a stupid old jersey but possession of his fascinating soul.

Jake closed the gap between them, searing his right hand to her left. She couldn't see him, but she sure could feel him. Vibrating heat rose like a restless fog between them. All at the same time, invisible yet omnipresent. So close but yet so far.

Touch me—all of me, her every instinct screamed.

I've missed you so bad. I've missed the happy-go-lucky spirit I used to be whenever you were around.

He slipped his hand beneath her chin, tipping it upward, curving his roving hand around her throat before covering her lips with his.

For a long second the world as Candy had known it stopped, then resumed a slow, lazy spinning. The kind of spinning little kids do on sun-drenched front lawns.

With Jake kissing her, birds and angels sang.

Cats and dogs united.

The whole universe had gone topsy-turvy mad and she, Candy Jacobs, stood at the very core with her heart pounding every bit as hard as it had during their first kiss on the Lonesome High football field all those years ago.

When he pulled away, she touched her fingers to her lips, testing to see if they were really swollen, testing to see if she was really awake or if this was just another of her heady dreams.

"Hello? Earth to Jacobs?"

Candy flinched when Jake waved his hand in front of her face.

"I, uh, forgot what I was saying."

"You were refusing to play nice by claiming you were going to keep my jersey."

"You really want it back?" she asked, hoping her question didn't come out sounding as panic-stricken as it felt. For if after that kiss, he wasn't feeling what she was—that maybe Saturday night was too long to wait to give him an answer, and that maybe they needed to ask a neighbor to watch Bonnie, then march their agreement right on up the stairs to their old bedroom where they could seal it with another kiss—she had much bigger problems than unexpected longing.

"What do you think?" he asked, sliding his hand to her chest, covering her pounding heart.

"What I think," she said, licking her lips, willing her pulse to slow, "is that you're teasing me. I think you never really wanted your jersey back, but were just angling for one more way to get beneath my skin."

"Did it work?"

She felt his grin.

"No. I was on to you all time."

"Bull."

WHILE JAKE GOT BONNIE dressed for her play date— an afternoon spent crawling with Warren and Franny's eight-month-old, Toby—Candy washed up the chili splotches Jake left on her counter, stove and best frying pan. As for the mess he'd made of her emotions, she wasn't quite sure how to handle that—especially the part where she knew she should have been upset with him for kissing her, but couldn't quite figure out why.

She'd always prided herself on her honesty, and honestly, she'd wanted that kiss.

She wanted that kiss from the moment Jake strolled through Candy Kisses' door on Monday afternoon. Why, she had no idea—and yes, that was true.

She suspected it had something to do with that sexy grin, maybe a little more with his delicious masculine scent. His eyes. That adorable crook in his nose. But more and more she was suspecting it was the way he cared for Bonnie. Walking in on the two of them sleeping in that recliner had flip-flopped her heart in a thousand tiny ways.

For all these years, she'd blamed him for breaking her heart. Had he been the one responsible? Or had she done the breaking all by herself?

Because as tough as Jake came across on the outside, those moments when she caught him smoothing Bonnie's hair, fixing the collars on one of her tiny dresses, or planting a kiss on top of her head, spoke louder than any words he ever could have spoken. Jake was no heartbreaker, for in taking poor, orphaned Bonnie into his home and arms, he was a *heart-mender.*

Maybe, just maybe, if she'd open herself to the possibility that what he'd said about her being nothing like her mom could be true, then her own heart could be mended, too?

Filling the sink with hot, sudsy water, the mere thought caused Candy's hands to tremble.

Just imagine, no more lonely nights, picking at rubbery TV dinners before reading the paper, doing a few lines of needlepoint, then retiring to her cold bed.

Closing her eyes, she thought back to what it had been like crawling into bed beside Jake.

He was so much bigger than her that when they spooned, snuggling against him she felt drawn into his strength. As though as long as she was safe in the cocoon of his arms, no outside pain could encroach.

"Okay, Candy Cane, we're outta here."

She jumped when Jake sauntered up behind her and planted a quick kiss on her cheek.

"Catch you on the flip side—and be dressed for a swim and sail. Me and you are gonna catch some rays." Holding Bonnie's hands high, he gently flapped her tiny arms as if she were waving. With Bonnie giggling, he said in a high falsetto, "'Bye-bye, Auntie Candy. Be sure you kiss Daddy lots for me while I'm gone. You know how bad he misses me.''

Laughing, Candy flicked suds at the both of them. "I thought you two comedians were leaving?"

"We are," Jake said. "Just as soon as I do this." He leaned forward to kiss her again, but this time, square on the lips, with enough heated pressure to buckle her knees. "There," he said, his satisfied expression not the least bit guilty. "Now, we can go."

And they did.

The second the front door closed and Candy stood at the kitchen window, watching Jake fasten Bonnie into her car seat, then hopping in behind the wheel and driving away, her life felt curiously empty again, the way it had before Jake had stormed back into her life.

Lips pressed tight, she scrubbed an already-clean coffee mug she'd meant to set on the top rack of the dishwasher.

What did these zinging butterflies in her tummy imply? Why, when in just a few days she was supposed to embark on the trip of a lifetime, was she much more looking forward to the prospect of an afternoon spent with Jake than seeing the ancient wonders of Peru?

And just when she finished worrying about all the mundane stuff, the really hard-hitting questions set in. Such as, what in the world was she going to wear? And the granddaddy of them all…

How was she going to hide Goldilocks?

"PUSH, KELLY! We've got to move faster or we'll never get it out in time."

"This is stupid," Kelly said. Out of breath, drenched in sweat, she plopped onto the three-legged gold corduroy couch that now sat half outside the boathouse and half in the blazing sun. "A genuine lamebrained home run."

"Got any better ideas?" Candy asked.

"Yeah, let's leave it here and maybe a freak tornado will carry the nasty old thing to the dump."

"Bite your tongue!" Candy said. "Jake and I spent

some unbelievable times on this sofa. I couldn't take it to the dump. It'd be like throwing away a part of the family. Quit bellyaching and help. Now, come on,'' Candy muttered, planting her hands beneath the far end. ''You push and I'll pull.''

''And then what?'' Kelly didn't budge from her cozy seat. ''Are you hoping the gold corduroy'll blend in with the grass? Or maybe you could hide it behind that dead azalea bush?''

''Kelly Foster, has anyone ever told you you're just plain mean?''

Candy's watery eyes felt dangerously close to spilling. ''*Please* help. What you don't know is, the first night Jake was in town, he asked about this couch, and I told him I did take it to the dump, so when he sees it, he's gonna know something is up.''

''Oh, I get it. Like if he sees this big gold monster, he's gonna know you still have the hots for him?''

''Sort of—only I don't.''

''Right.''

''Well, I don't. I'm just sentimental about certain things. That's all.''

''Sentimental about what things?'' Jake asked, whistling around the corner of the whitewashed boathouse before stopping dead in his tracks. ''Well, I'll be damned,'' he said, casting Candy a heated stare. ''Looks to me like a certain ex-wife of mine has some explaining to do.''

Kelly rolled her eyes. ''I've gotta get to work. Please, Jake, before I get home at five, ravage Candy senseless on this couch, then marry her quick before the great sex daze wears off.''

"Will do," Jake said, waving as Kelly bounded up the hill.

Beyond mortified and entering the realm of praying for alien abduction, Candy wilted onto the couch, cradling her face in her hands.

Jake plopped down beside her, gallantly slipping his arm around her shoulders. "Tell me, Mrs. Peterson, what's it like getting caught in one of your own lies?"

"I go by the name of *Ms. Jacobs* now, thank you very much. And I didn't lie." Her voice came out muffled, her face still being hidden behind her hands.

"Oh, yeah? What exactly is this we're sitting on then? Goldilocks' long lost twin?" Without waiting for her reply, he stretched his endless legs in front of him, crossing them at the ankles before lacing his hands behind his head. "Damn, we had some great times on this couch. I'll bet to this day nobody in this whole town has tried out some of the positions we—"

"Honestly, Jake! Do you mind?"

"Repeating a few of them for old times' sake? Hell no, I don't mind."

"You know full well what I mean, so kindly get that smirk off your face."

"What smirk? This is a grin of happiness. Yup," he said, stretching out on the far end and taking her, shrieking all the way, along for the ride. "This is my idea of fun."

"Jake? Are you crazy?"

"For you."

"You've already used that line once this week," she said, trying to ignore the fact that Jake hugged her against his chest. With the heat of the sun on her back and the even hotter heat of his chest warming her breasts, she scarcely found air to breathe, let alone to say, "What's the matter, too lazy to think up a new line?"

"Nope, just no need."

"I'm not worth the extra creativity?"

"No. It's just that I'm way too busy thinking about how good it'll feel doing this…" Fingers splayed on the back of her head, he pressed her lips to his. With their heads on the end of the couch in the shade and their midsections exposed to the sun, Candy wasn't sure whether the pulsing between her legs had something to do with Jake or impending sunstroke.

Either way, after what felt like fifty years of long, cold winter, she figured it was a wonderful way to go.

Jake stirred beneath her, pressing his arousal against the very spot screaming for his attention.

"No, Jake," she said, her voice wispy, breaths ragged. "We can't do this. It wouldn't be right."

"Why?" He kissed her even harder. "I want you. I'm guessing you want me. We're back on Goldilocks—which I'm assuming you've saved for just such an occasion. Looks to me like all systems are go."

"But we're outside. Just anyone could—"

"Who, Candy? It's the middle of the week. Not a fisherman in sight. All the neighborhood kids seem to be inside." He kissed her hard again. "And you know damned well from previous experience that no one can see down here unless they're standing at one of our bedroom windows.''

''What if we have a burglar?''

Jake laughed. ''Then I guess he or she will get quite an eyeful.''

Candy wanted to fight him, the very idea of surrendering herself to him all over again. Of opening up to the pain of losing him all over again. But in the end, her need was too strong.

She wanted him with a yearning that all at once made her happy and sad. She wanted him with every breath, every beat of her heart.

And so she pushed herself upright, sitting tall and proud, raking the scrunchie from her ponytail, fanning her hair into a silky black curtain she drapped around her shoulders. Next, before Jake's sex-sleepy eyes, she dragged her white sleeveless T-shirt over her head and flung it to the daisy-strewn grass. Beneath her shirt, she wore a white bikini top she never would have dared to wear in public if Kelly hadn't talked her into it.

After untying the strings at the neck, she cinched open the back clasp, still cupping the flimsy scrap to her full breasts. ''A-are you sure we should be doing this?''

Jake nodded. ''Woman, this is what I've dreamed of every night we've been apart.'' Struggling to where he was sitting up, too, he cradled her on his lap and eased her legs around his waist.

So excited, yet so afraid that she actually trembled, she clung to him, and he held her tight, only releasing her for the moment it took to tug his own T-shirt over his head. Then he was back, crushing her breasts to his chest. His coarse hair grazed the tender flesh, reminding her that he was all hard muscle to her soft curves.

She wore cutoffs and beneath those, her bikini bottom. "I want you," she said. "Now."

"Shh," he said, murmuring a whispered kiss to her fevered lips. "Not so fast. We've got all day. Let's use it."

Chapter Nine

Jake slid Candy from his lap to the free end of the couch. His hand on the small of her back, he eased her down, down into white-hot sun.

Her nipples puckered and ached for him, and he answered their call by sucking and nipping. Laving and kneading. And when he'd had his fill of one, he claimed the other, while all the while, she relearned the feel of him on her palms. The feel of his smooth, angular back, hair-coarsened, rippled stomach and chest. Hair she raked her fingers through, closing them into fists when he dragged needy moans past her lips.

"Please," she said, thrashing her head back and forth, feeling as if she were rocking though all of her was planted solidly on terra firma. Gentle waves lapped the pebbled shore. Jake lapped from her navel as if supping on sweet nectar.

And then he unbuttoned her shorts, slid them down.

He did the same with her bikini bottom, tossing them both beyond her line of sight.

A cloud passed over the sun, for a second, stealing

her heat. But Jake, ever the gentleman, lent her his own heat, not taking long, but yet taking an eternity to remove his swim trunks.

Easing her legs apart, he played in the nest between them, hiding a finger there, licking here, building crazy bonfires within her that crackled with restless heat. "Please, Jake," she urged, fisting her hands in his hair as she bucked and moaned against him.

Just when she felt near bursting with intangible need, he entered her, swift and sure, setting up a rhythm as old as time. "I've wanted this—you, for such a long time," he said, bracing one hand on the back of the sofa, the other on the cushion beside her head. "Please, don't ever make me wait this long again."

"No," she said, her voice raspy and deep. "No, I won't. Never again."

And then there was no room for words when all that was left between them was raw emotion.

In and out.

In and out.

She met him thrust for thrust, washing her hands over his sweat-slick chest. In and out. In and out. He thrust harder now, which was good, because she needed him more now. Deeper. Harder.

Magic was building, spreading, towering into blazing heat that battled the sun and won. "Jake, I—"

"I know—me, too."

He squeezed his eyes shut tight.

Flinched, groaned.

Her toes curled in pleasure, and she tossed her head back in thoroughly reckless abandon.

They kissed, celebrating their reunion, release, re-commitment to what once was, and what might, if they both tread carefully, forever more be.

HOURS LATER, her bikini back on, Candy lounged on the small wooden sailboat deck. ''Mmm,'' she said, soaking in the sun. ''I could get used to days like this.''

''Me, too,'' Jake said. ''Does this mean you've made your decision? That you will be headed back to Florida with me?''

Her heart lurched.

She wanted to.

Oh, how she wanted to, but even after what the two of them just shared, there was still a part of her terrified to make another commitment. Terrified of making another mistake. ''Please, Jake, don't press me. Don't spoil this perfect day. I just need more time.''

Cradling her head in his lap, he smoothed hair back from her forehead. ''Beauty, you've got all the time in the world—as long as you get back to me by Saturday night.''

''Deal,'' she said, not only grateful for the time, but for his understanding.

''YOU'RE SO MAKING THAT UP,'' Candy said a short while later on a sandy beach across the lake from her house. Licking squirt cheese and cracker crumbs from her fingers, she added, ''Never once did I ask Kelly to spy on you back in high school. Now 'round about the fourth year we were married, when you said you were working all those extra hours, but were never at the store when I called, then I put her to work.''

He sat up on his elbows. ''Then you knew all along what I was up to that Christmas? The rocker wasn't a surprise?''

Swallowing hard, she shook her head. ''I was so afraid you were seeing another woman.''

''Why?'' he asked, sliding his hand beneath the fall of her damp hair. They'd gone for a brief swim, but when they quickly found the water was still much too cold, they'd opted for a beach picnic instead. ''What would have ever given you that idea?''

She shrugged. The usual suspects. Insecurity. Fear. ''You talked so much about having kids, and then when you actually gave me the rocker, that made it even worse, because I knew the dreams of us becoming a family that'd prompted you to make it.''

Heart surprisingly heavy, Jake summoned the courage to ask, ''I, uh, don't suppose you still have it?''

''Of course I still have it,'' she said, looking as if he'd hurt her to even ask. ''It's in the attic beneath a special cover I made to keep away the dust.''

''You're kidding?''

''Why would I kid about something so serious? I always knew that one day you were destined to become a dad, Jake. Even if the two of us never had children together, that didn't mean you wouldn't have them someday, with…some other woman. It was only a matter of time, so I saved the chair for you. For your children.''

Candy's admission rocked Jake to his core. ''You're amazing. Did you know that?''

She dropped her glance. "Nonsense. I just did what any caring person would do."

Jake shook his head. "I have to admit, when you first told me that you'd in a sense not so much as divorced me, but let me go so I'd be free to marry another woman, that a part of me thought it was a load of bull. I mean, come on, *let me go?* Nobody's that altruistic. Nobody, that is, except for you, Candy Jacobs-Peterson." Leaning across the blanket, he kissed her, soft at first, then gradually increasing the urgency as, with his hand behind her head, he gently lowered her to the time-softened flannel blanket.

"I want to make love to you again," he said, meeting her lidded, whiskey-brown gaze.

She nodded, slipped her hands behind his head to pull his lips to hers. Jake cupped her exquisite face in his hands, committing the sight of her to memory.

What if she turned him down Saturday night?

Sure, he'd told himself he was only in Lonesome to find a mom for Bonnie, but why was it that more and more he felt as if he also wanted a wife for himself—and not just any wife, but *his* wife—Candy.

The whole notion was nuts.

Today, easily explained away by his having spent too much time in the sun. Because really, he no more wanted a wife than Candy wanted a husband.

With his index finger, he traced her collarbone.

She shivered.

"You cold?" he asked, voice filled with concern.

She shook her head. "Just excited…and more than a little scared."

"Of what?" he asked, tracing her eyebrows.

"Us. This. Where does it end, Jake? How did it even begin?"

"Does any of that really matter? Can't we just play it by ear?"

"You're right. I'm getting ahead of myself."

"Absolutely," he said with a kiss. "No decisions of any kind until Saturday."

"Yeah, but that is only one day away."

"True, but think how much living we can squeeze into that twenty-four hours."

"Mmm, twenty-four decision-free hours. I do like the sound of that."

"Me, too. Wanna celebrate?"

"What did you have in mind?"

"Oh, maybe a little of this," he said, pressing openmouthed kisses to her sun-warmed chest. "And definitely a whole lot of that." He'd slipped his hand beneath her bikini top, toying with her already hard nipple.

Closing her eyes to the fathomless blue sky, Candy surrendered any lingering fear to an all-encompassing, ever-growing need to once again travel with Jake on the most exquisite journey two people could take.

A journey of minds and bodies.

Hearts and souls.

She'd been looking for that elusive something for such a long time, yet here, in Jake's arms, she felt complete.

Complete?

The very idea was so unexpected, so foreign, Candy wasn't sure what to do with it. So, in the end, she filed it for safekeeping, then surrendered herself to the wild ride to come.

ON THE SHORT VOYAGE home, Jake sat comfortably on the sole of his baby, the turn-of-the-century Seabright skiff he'd coerced Candy into buying on their first vacation to Maine. After having spent almost a year restoring it to its former glory, he'd hated losing it to divorce almost as much as Candy, but lose it he had, just like his football jersey, just like that box of love letters she'd pushed at him—and he'd rejected—on his last trip out the front door.

Looking back, his pride had been the one telling him it'd be easier to walk away than to speak to Candy about arranging for the boat's transport, even though the fifteen-foot craft could have easily enough been put on its trailer.

After not seeing the boat for ten years, he was amazed to have found it in such great shape, deeply touched when Candy admitted to having had an old carpenter friend of theirs regularly sand and revarnish the hundred-year-old mahogany planks.

Leaning against the tiller, his back resting against the helm, his woman asleep with her head on his lap, rare peace overcame him.

Maybe it was the rhythmic lapping of waves on the clinker-built hull? Maybe it was the rich scent of sun-warmed water? The wind in his hair? The ocean of blue sky? Sure, any one of those things could be responsible for making him feel this good, but deep down, he suspected his peace had more to do with Bonnie and the fact that because Candy would certainly agree to his proposal, he'd never again face the sheer terror of what it might feel like to be forced to give up his child.

DRESSING FOR DINNER later that night, Candy clutched her queasy tummy. Were a couple dozen moths throwing a keg party in there?

If only Kelly could help select the perfect dreamy outfit. But seeing how her relationship radar would lock in on the fact that Candy had done more that afternoon that just sail with Jake, Candy wouldn't have dreamed of asking her friend over.

Although why was she worried about Kelly knowing when in under an hour everyone in town would know when Jake, Bonnie and her showed up at Digger's Barbecue for dinner!

Glancing at her face in the bathroom mirror, Candy frowned, but even making a face did nothing to extinguish the glow. The great sex glow she hadn't sported in say, oh, about ten years!

Hands to her cheeks, she said, "Oh, my gosh, this afternoon Jake and I really made love! Eek!" After a quick and quiet happy dance, she fairly skipped out of the bathroom and back to her closet.

A knock sounded on her bedroom door. "Candy?" Jake asked, the thick oak muffling his voice. "Can I come in?"

She glanced down at her skimpy bra and panties before blazing with a deep blush. "Uh, sure. Just a second."

Too late.

In customary Jake style, he barged right in. "Oops.

Sorry.'' Making no attempt to head back from whence he'd came, he appraised her with a slow whistle. ''I take that back. I'm not in the least bit sorry. Why not just wear that tonight? I'm sure you'd be a big hit.''

She reached to the bed for two pillows. One to cover herself with, and the other to pitch at Jake!

''Hey, watch it!'' he said. ''And here I am bearing gifts.'' He brought a shiny black box out from behind his back. It'd been tied with the distinct pink ribbon of Amanda Perkins's dress shop—the most expensive store in town.

''What's in there?'' she asked, stepping a smidgen closer.

''Oh, so you do like presents?''

''Just a little.'' She grinned, holding up her thumb and forefinger, then pinching them together.

He shook the box. ''If you want it, you'll have to come get it.''

''Never,'' she teased.

''Okay, then, guess I'll have to take this stunning garment back to the store.''

''Oh, I wouldn't do that,'' she said. ''Surely we can work out a compromise?''

He took a moment to think. ''Might it involve making use of that big bed of yours for something other than sleeping?''

She blushed all the more. ''You're bad.''

''Hmm, you didn't seem to mind that fact this afternoon.''

''Just give me the box,'' she said, lunging for it. But he was quicker and before she could say ''kiss me quick,'' he'd done just that, flopping her giggling and breathless onto the bed, before thoroughly kissing the fight right out of her.

''There, that's what I'll give you,'' he said.

''Mmm, I like it. Got any more?''

''For you, I've got plenty more where that came from.'' Again he pressed his lips to hers, but this time for a leisurely exploration, parting her lips with his tongue, inviting hers out onto the happening dance floor of the Getting Reacquainted Lounge. ''Oh, you taste good,'' he said on a groan, sliding his big hand along the hourglass of her hips, waist and breasts.

''You, too.''

''So? You want to skip going out for dinner and dine in?''

From down the hall came the furtive sniffles and cries of Bonnie waking from her nap.

Jake groaned. ''Just my luck she wakes up right when things are getting good.''

''Duty calls,'' Candy said. ''Want me to get her?''

''No, what I want you to do,'' he said, planting one last kiss on the tip of her nose before pushing himself off of her and onto his feet, ''is to pour yourself into the contents of that box.''

''Yes, sir,'' she said, sending him a jaunty salute from her post in the center of the now lonely bed.

From the door he added, ''And don't even think about wearing your hair up.''

''I THOUGHT I told you not to wear your hair up?'' Jake said from behind his water glass. They'd long since eaten Digger's world-famous ribs and now occupied a loft table at Candy Kisses, waiting for ice-cream sundaes.

Candy, still radiant in her new curve-hugging coral sundress flashed him a sassy wink. "Do you think just because you tell me to do something, that means I'm automatically going to do it?"

"A man can dream, can't he?"

She rolled her eyes before turning her attention to Bonnie. "How're you doing, sweetie?"

The baby held out her chubby arms, pinching her fingers in the sign that she wanted Candy to pick her up.

"She's fine," Jake said, unwrapping a packet of saltines he'd snatched from her diaper bag and placing them on Bonnie's high-chair tray. Once the infant put a cracker to her mouth, he said, "I'm the one in agony from composing this mental list of all the ways I could set your hair free. And after doing that, I'd need to remove that damned dress, too, because looking at it on the window mannequin, I thought it'd show a whole lot more skin than it really does."

"Honestly, Jake," she said, pressing her hand over her heaving bosom, courtesy of the matching black push-up bra and panties he'd also been thoughtful enough to supply. "If I show any more skin, someone's going to have the sheriff arrest me."

He leaned close, kissing the curve between her neck and shoulder blade. "Mmm, arrest…handcuffs…strip searching…this just keeps getting better."

"Would you hush," Candy said, glancing around the crowded room to see if anyone had heard. They hadn't, and it looked as if none of their fellow dessert eaters even cared.

Oddly enough, everyone present in the six-table loft looked to be from out of town—not a particularly unusual occurrence, but one for which Candy was especially thankful tonight.

It was hard sitting in what was soon to be someone else's business, being served by the new owner's two oldest sons, all the while knowing their parents had taken her place downstairs at the counter—just for practice so they'd know the routine once the sale papers were signed. Throwing Jake into the mix would have by itself made for an amazingly difficult night, but now it had turned into an all-out stressfest.

"How are you holding up?" he asked.

"I'm okay."

"Liar." He handed Bonnie another cracker.

"All right, so this whole setup gives me the creeps. Usually, I'm the one dashing around, scooping ice cream, squirting whipped cream, making sure everyone has full glasses of iced tea, soda pop and coffee. This just doesn't feel right, sitting here being waited on when I should be down there working my buns off."

"If you don't like being waited on, why are you selling?"

She sighed. "Haven't we been over this like a thousand times?"

"Since you won't let me pull you into some dark closet and ravage you senseless, I've got nothing better to do. Let's make it a thousand and one."

One of the Hammond boys, nine-year-old twin,

Jerry, set heaping banana splits on their table. "My brother Terry'll be back to refill your colas." He was about to leave, then turned back. "Almost forgot. Need extra napkins?"

"No, thanks," Candy said.

"Okay, then—'bye," Jerry said, flashing them a harried smile.

"Cute kid," Jake said, feeding Bonnie a spoonful of whipped cream. "You know, you'd make a fortune franchising this place. It has a nice, old-fashioned vibe. Can you imagine if family-style sit-down candy and ice-cream shops like this were on every street corner like McDonald's? Good food, along with real conversation instead of drive-thru car chitchat."

Nodding, Candy swallowed hard.

"Hey," Jake said, covering her hand with his. "I meant all of that as a compliment. Adding this ice-cream parlor to Candy Kisses was a great idea."

"Thanks."

Terry refilled their drinks.

After thanking the boy and slipping him a tip to share with his brother, Jake asked Candy, "So? What's your problem?" Not waiting for an answer, he popped his cherry into her mouth, holding on to the stem. His sweet gesture hardly put her more at ease, especially since she used to teasingly beg for his cherry and he teasingly refused. Now he was all of a sudden offering one of his own free will?

"My problem is…" she said, "is that I came here tonight expecting to at least handle a few disasters, but look how smoothly everything's going. No running out of whipped cream or Coco Locos. No overly sticky kids. The pop dispenser hasn't even broken down. It's as if no one ever needed me around here.''

"That's not true," Jake said. "And how do you know complete pandemonium isn't breaking out in the kitchen where, from the smell of it, Betsy's baking chocolate chip cookies?''

"Oh, great. I'm not even gone yet and already she's adding homemade cookies to my menu.'' Frowning, she added, "It's not even that I want anything bad to happen, I just…''

"Want to feel a little more needed?''

Swiping at teary eyes, she nodded.

"If it helps, *I* need you. And Bonnie definitely needs you.'' They looked in unison at the baby who had smeared her angelic face with whipped cream, strawberry topping and chocolate ice cream. "And there's your overly sticky kid right here.'' She'd even globbed cracker crumbs onto her grinning cheeks.

Candy couldn't help but smile.

"That's better,'' Jake said, bringing her hand to his lips before flipping it to tenderly kiss her palm. "You told me when I first came to town that you felt as if you were missing a part of yourself.''

"Yeah, so?''

"So…'' he said, gesturing to their surroundings. To the pine-paneled walls covered in antiques, to the pressed-tin ceiling, the rag-rugged floors, the low din of happy conversation over the strums of gentle blue-grass being played by a local band loving the free exposure.

"Did it ever occur to you to look for this missing

link of yours not in some foreign place like the Andes, but in here?''

His covering her heart with his big hand caused a dizzying array of heat and confusion.

''I—I don't know what you mean,'' she said, toying with her melting swirl of ice cream and toppings.

''What I mean,'' he said, taking her spoon from her hand, setting it on her plate, then raising her chin to force her to meet his gaze, ''is that maybe what you're missing is family. You've told me this uneasiness of yours started about the time your grandfather died. What if you feel lost because six days and four nights of the week, you see families operating the way they're supposed to. But then you go home to that big old empty house of yours, and see the perfect backdrop we made for our family—yours and mine— the family that evidently was never meant to be.''

''Stop,'' she said, eyes brimming with tears. ''My leaving Lonesome and selling Candy Kisses has nothing to do with family. The whole idea's absurd.''

''Why? Because that hurt little girl inside of you is always butting into your business by telling you you're not worthy of having a family? That you don't deserve one? Well, I'm here to tell you that that just ain't so. Look around, Candy Cane. See all these smiling people? Just once, open yourself up to the possibility of becoming one of them—happy I mean.'' He leaned conspiratorially close. ''Okay— correction. Transformation is good unless you change yourself into ugly old Bean Harbow down there.''

Heart pounding, she grinned in the direction of his gaze. Bean Harbow had been given his name because his wife claimed he cared nothin' about beans except for playin' his fiddle. Dressed in overalls, wearing a blissful smile and more white hair on his face than his head, Candy didn't think he looked all that bad. At least he knew what he wanted to do with his life.

"Wh-what are you saying?" she asked, trying to be casual by licking chocolate sauce from her spoon.

"What I'm saying is—first off, quit that licking. You look sexy as hell." As if to clear it, he shook his head before briefly looking away.

Candy lowered her spoon.

"Thank you. Now, what I was trying to say is that if only you'd agree to marry me, you, me and Bonnie—we could start our own family. For the next year the three of us'll be this happy every night. Just think, no more long, lonely nights of needlepointing or crocheting those butt-ugly blanket thingees."

"Hey, I happen to think those hand-crocheted afghan *thingees* are pretty. When I was six years old, my grandpa taught me how to make them."

"Your grandpa taught you?" Jake made a face. "He struck me as being more manly than that. We watched John Wayne movies together."

"Hey, he and Grandma used to work on them while watching John Wayne movies together. Then they gave them to charities. How else do you think he learned?"

Wielding his dangerously sexy grin, the one that made his velvety-brown eyes crinkle at the corners while unwittingly melting her heart, he said, "Okay, so you teach me how to make those ugly hand-crocheted afghan *thingees* and just like your grandma

and grandpa, we'll crochet together.'' He fixed her
with a curiously direct gaze. One that sent her al-
ready-churning stomach into a whole new fit of ups
and downs. "All kidding aside, Candy…come on,
what do you say? Marry me. Tomorrow. Hell, for that
matter—tonight. Right now. Let's drive to Branson.''

Jake studied her face, the way anger at first flashed
in her dark eyes before her expression softened, and
all he could do was pray she was caving in.

"Candy?'' he said, squeezing her hands. "Please
don't leave me hanging.''

"All of that togetherness sounds real nice,'' she
said, releasing a breath of air. "But what about the
realities? What happens when a year from now, we're
still great at not only making blankets, but fooling
around under them? But just like the first time we
tried marriage, what happens when you start hounding
me with the same old questions? What then, Jake?
How happy are we going to be then?''

Sighing, she toyed with the muddy glop that had
been her dessert. "I want to believe you when you
make all of these pretty predictions about our future.
Truly, I do. But I'm scared. So damned scared of
making another mistake. And as hard as it was to get
over you the first time… Honestly, I don't know if
my heart can withstand that kind of pain all over
again.''

Chapter Ten

Hours after tucking Bonnie into her crib, Jake was still tossing and turning.

What was Candy thinking?

Did she regret putting him off yet again? Even worse, did she regret his ever coming back to town?

This afternoon he thought all of his problems had been solved, but now it seemed maybe they weren't. What would it take to make Candy see that not only would she make a great temporary wife, but mom?

He'd tried the whole reverse-psychology thing and aside from keeping him in town, it hadn't performed any relationship miracles. Besides which, if Candy ever knew just how right she'd been in her assessment that his whole football-field reenactment of their first date had been a setup designed to remind her how close they used to be, she'd come unglued. At least now there was a chance she'd say yes Saturday night.

Yup, the way he saw it, the best way to go about ensuring Candy agreed to his proposal was to follow his same course. Given one more idyllic day like today, surely she'd see the short-term potential the two of them shared? Surely, surely, she'd see?

AT 3:16 A.M. Candy had had all she could take of tossing and turning. She threw back her light comforter, crept to the door and slowly opened it, hoping that just this once it wouldn't creak.

She winced at the jarring sound in the quiet hall. Rats. So much for those positive hopes.

Looking one way, then the other, she crept to Bonnie's room, guided by slivers of moonlight peeking through the open doors of the three other rooms. Thankfully, Jake occupied the guest room at the top of the stairs, meaning at least she didn't have to pass by him.

She found Bonnie curled on her belly with her covers rumpled clear on the other side of the crib. A chilly breeze stirred lace curtains at the open window, carrying in dampness from the lake.

Pressing her fingers to Bonnie's chubby legs and arms, Candy frowned to find a rampant crop of goose bumps. She gently turned the baby onto her back, covered her with a soft flannel blanket, then tucked on the heavier baby-comforter before closing the window.

For the longest time, resting her elbows on the top of the crib rail, Candy stared at Bonnie, memorizing the curve of her tiny nose and forehead, eyebrows and cheeks. The sleeping angel was perfect. And just think, if Candy dared, this living, breathing miracle could be hers every day for a whole year.

But what then?

What happened at year's end when Jake told her it was time to go home? Could she bear the pain?

On the flip side, could she bear the pain of losing Bonnie now? And not just Bonnie, but Jake?

The last thing Candy had planned to do was to make love with him, but what a wonderful surprise that turned out to be. The valleys and peaks he'd carried her to had stolen her breath. Drowned her in sun-drenched curiosity for what their future might hold.

Yet at the same time, suspicion filled her with wary dread. Could Jake have seen their lovemaking as nothing more than a pleasant way to fill an otherwise dull afternoon? Or was it possible that he, too, had seen it as the promise of something more?

Pressing her fingers to heart throbbing temples, Candy prayed for answers that wouldn't come.

Bonnie fitfully stirred.

Candy knew she should probably encourage her back to sleep, but she instead scooped the infant into her arms, blankets and all.

"Hey, sweetie," Candy crooned. "What's the matter? Have a bad dream?" Bonnie pressed her cheek to the swell of Candy's breasts, stirring a fierce, confusing longing.

Cradling her close, Candy stood in front of the window, gently rocking, staring at the moonlit diamonds strewn across the lake.

She thought of Jake's rocking chair, the one he'd made for her to rock their child to sleep in this very spot.

A glance at Bonnie showed that she was once again

sound asleep. Candy eased her back into her crib and tucked her in again before heading for the door.

Creeping down the hall, she came to the attic door, opened it, and flipped the switch that illuminated all three forty-watt bulbs before gingerly making her way up squeaky stairs.

At the top, she weaved through boxes labeled Fat Clothes and Skinny Clothes and Christmas Ornaments and Halloween Costumes. Antique dressers and side tables and chairs she'd always planned to refinish but hadn't yet found the time added to the treachery of the dimly lit trail.

Miles of memories later, she found the rocker just where she'd stashed it after the divorce, tucked safely beneath a handmade calico cover—along with teaching her to crochet, her grandfather had also taught her to sew.

She slipped off the cover, then lugged the chair between still more boxes and what she warily knew to be a chest of her mother's old clothes. Even after safely making it past that perilous spot in the trail, Candy soon discovered that although the rocker appeared deceptively light, it weighed as much as a cast-iron stove!

A pile of three boxes crashed to the floor, causing a domino effect with a lamp that'd been set upon a side table that'd been set atop a leaning buffet.

"Candy? That you up there?"

Great.

The commotion woke the one person in the world she didn't want to see. What happened to Jake sleeping like the dead? And why couldn't that be one thing about him that hadn't changed?

"Uh, yes. It's me."

The narrow stairs groaned beneath his footfalls. "What are you doing?" he asked, scratching his whisker-shadowed jaw. "It's after four in the morning."

"And your point is?"

He froze at the top of the stairs, fixing her with a tight grin. "Need help?"

"I can manage."

"From the looks of the wreckage you're leaving in your wake, I'm thinking maybe you can't." In an instant he wove through the mess to stand at her side.

He was only wearing navy boxers dotted with tiny baseballs and bats. When she'd gone to bed, it'd been too hot for the bottoms so she'd only donned the tank T-shirt that matched her cat print pajamas. She now wished she'd pulled them on. Tugging at the shirt hem would have been pointless, so she made do with crossing her arms.

"Really, Jake, I've got this handled."

"If you wanted the rocker down from the attic, all you had to do was ask."

"I know. But I didn't know I wanted it until just a little while ago. Bonnie seemed restless and I thought it might be nice to rock her back to sleep."

"Sure. That's what I made the rocker for." He inched past her, brushing thigh against thigh, arm against arm.

Aching awareness of him, and of how much closer

they'd been that afternoon, stirred a familiar longing deep within her.

As if it weighed no more than Bonnie, Jake hefted the chair above the boxes and took a different route to the stairs. "Coming?" he asked, flashing her a look over his shoulder.

"Uh, yeah." *Just as soon as I finish studying those tree trunks you call arms!* She licked suddenly dry lips, then chased down the stairs after him.

"I'm assuming you want this in the nursery?" he asked in the hall.

"Yes."

"Cool."

In the baby's room, he set the chair in front of the bay window that overlooked the lake.

He gestured for Candy to have a seat, but she said, "No, you have the first rock. After all, you made it."

"True, but I made it for you."

"Do you always have to be so argumentative?" she asked, trying unbelievably hard to look anywhere but at his unbelievable pecs.

"And here I thought I was merely being polite."

"Fine," she said. "I'll rock first."

"Thank you."

"You're welcome."

The chair sat like a dream.

Just like everything Jake put his hands to creating, the word perfection didn't begin to do the rocker justice. The intricately scrolled arms felt silky-smooth to the touch and the rockers fairly purred against the hardwood floor.

"Oh, Jake," she said, hating that for all these years

bitterness and stubborn pride had caused her to keep this work of art hidden in the dusty old attic. "It's beautiful. How can I ever thank you?"

Placing a sleeping Bonnie in her arms, Jake stood back and smiled. "You just did."

"What do you mean?"

"Seeing you, holding my baby in the chair I made for this very purpose. That's all the thanks I'll ever need."

"WHAT DO YOU WANT to do today?" Jake asked over chili-cheese toast on Friday morning.

Candy took one look at the plate he'd prepared for her, and said, "Not to hurt your feelings, but I'd say first on my list is to take a prebreakfast antacid."

"That's funny. But seriously, try it. It's pretty good stuff."

She forked a small bite, then tentatively raised it to her lips. "I don't know, Jake. Don't you know any breakfast recipes that don't call for chili?"

"What would be the point?" he asked, scooping a heaping forkful from his plate. "A morning without chili might as well be skipped."

Chewing while at the same time wrinkling her nose, Candy said, "Speaking of skipped, this is one of those mornings." She pushed back her chair from the table, stood, then reached for her plate.

"Where are you going?"

"To the disposal."

"Candy? I'm crushed."

"Good, then you and your icky-blicky breakfast'll

soon have something in common.'' On her way to the garbage disposal, she pressed a kiss to his forehead.

''Woman, you're cold.''

''No, just hungry.'' After dumping the contents of her plate into the sink, she poured a cup of coffee, added cream and sugar, then headed to the pantry to rummage through the vast supply of junk food Jake had steadily carted into the house. ''Funny how I'm supposed to be clearing this kitchen, but more and more stuff keeps coming in.''

''Speaking of which,'' he said through another bite, ''I bought you a pack of Nutter Butter. You still like 'em, right?''

Eyeing the unopened plastic pack of pure peanut butter bliss, she groaned. ''Are you trying to fatten me up?''

''Hey, there's nothing wrong with a woman who's got a little junk in her trunk.''

''Ah,'' she said with a laugh on her way back to the table. ''I knew there was a reason I've always loved you.''

''You've always loved me, huh? Even after the divorce?''

''Well…'' Her stomach lurched. What could she say?

After ten years of convincing herself maybe she'd never loved him, in just one short week she feared he and Bonnie occupied an alarming amount of space in her heart. Which was wrong, because even after the wonderful times they'd shared, that still didn't make her any better suited to becoming a wife or mother. As for love, previous experience taught her she didn't even know the meaning of the word. Clearing her throat, she said, ''Let's just say I'll always hold a certain affection for you and leave it at that.''

''Fair enough,'' he said, taking yet another bite of his foul concoction. ''So? You never did answer me. What's on schedule for today?''

She nibbled her lower lip, twirled locks of her hair. ''I, uh, really should spend the day at Candy Kisses, don't you think?'' *Because if I spend another day with you, who knows what could happen?* The rocking chair episode had proved that even the most seemingly innocent turn of events could wreak major havoc on her resolve.

Pushing his plate aside, Jake reached for her hands. ''Here's what I think we ought to do...''

''O-okay...'' No fair! He was aiming that dangerously sexy grin straight at her and darned if it wasn't working. Bending her will. Making her feel as if fulfilling his every wish was her one and only desire.

''I thought we'd start off by packing another picnic lunch...'' As he spoke, he rubbed the sensitive web of skin between her thumb and forefinger, strumming a low flame. ''Then we could head by the store and pick up one of those baby backpacks. It'd be good for the squirt to spend a day communing with nature, don't you think?''

The heat. The dull, throbbing ache between her legs.

Must stay strong.

Must resist *ever* again being alone with Jake.

''What if she gets bit by a tick or mosquito? Even worse, the copperheads are waking up.''

"Believe me, the snakes will hear us coming from miles away. And to make you happy, we'll get some bug spray at the store, too."

"Isn't it harmful for babies?"

He made a face. "Give me a break. I'm gonna rub it on her arms and legs and nose—not feed it to her."

His plan sounded safe—entirely *too* safe. Which meant, like his seemingly innocent day of sailing, Candy was already an emotional goner.

"I don't know, Jake. I really should make more Coco Locos for the store. Don't you think it'd be the neighborly thing to do?"

"Oh, and like entertaining me and Bonnie, your revered out-of-town guests, isn't neighborly?"

"It's not the same and you know it."

"Of course I do," he said, pulling her into a maddeningly cozy bear hug. "But do you think I'd ever admit it?"

EASING HIS BORING white rental sedan up to Galaxy Sports, Jake said, "How 'bout you and Bonnie stay in the car? I'll just be a sec getting her backpack."

"That's okay," Candy said. "I don't mind going in. Besides, I want to talk to Mona about what she's wearing Saturday night. She does still work in the golf department, doesn't she?"

He nodded. Swallowed hard.

What was he so jacked up about? Surely his guys had enough couth to realize they shouldn't go spilling break room strategy sessions to the very woman they'd been about?

"Okay, sure," he said, already reaching into the

back seat to unfasten the munchkin. "But skip the extended chitchat. I want to spend as much time as possible in the woods and it takes an hour just to drive to the trail."

"I know, I know," she said, grabbing her purse before climbing out of the car. "Good grief, you've only been a dad for a month, and already you're starting to lecture."

In the store Candy took Bonnie to see Mona while Jake jogged toward the backpacks.

"Candy!" Mona called when Candy reached Women's Golf Wear. In two seconds her old friend was crushing both her and the baby in a welcoming hug. "And hi there, Bonnie," she said, stepping back to pinch the baby's cheeks. "It's good to see you again, sweetie."

"Jake's had her at the store, huh?"

"Oh, yeah," Mona said, dumping a box of hot-pink golf balls into a cardboard display case. "First day Jake and this little lady rolled into town, while I baby-sat, he and the boys holed up in the break room dreaming up schemes to get you to marry him again."

"Oh?" Candy squeezed Bonnie extra hard.

"From what I've heard, after you initially kicked Jake out of your shop, he phased directly into Plan B, which was—according to Dietz—reverse psychology. Good thing you're such a smart cookie and would never even think of falling for such a ridiculous thing, huh?"

"Yeah. Good thing." Was it too much to ask to drop dead? At the very least, if Candy hadn't been holding Bonnie, she could have dived beneath the golf balls and never come out!

She'd known better than to trust Jake. She'd known better, but just like always, had listened to her heart instead of her head.

"What brings you by?" Mona asked.

Candy explained about the baby backpack, then, trying to sound as if her whole world hadn't just been shattered, asked Mona what she was wearing Saturday night.

"I bought this silver-sequined number in Kansas City," she said. "It fits *real* tight. Holds my boobs up and butt and gut in."

"Sounds nice," Candy said, only half listening.

"How about you?"

"I'm, uh, not quite sure yet. Heck," she said with a strangled laugh. "At this point, I'm not even sure if I'm going."

"You have to," Mona said. Leaning close, she whispered, "You didn't hear this from me, but Kelly's cooking up a plan to rig the king and queen vote so that you and Jake win. She's going around telling everyone that she single-handedly got the two of you back together, but I don't believe it for a second. If you decide to help Jake with this custody thing, it'll be because that's just the kind of person you are—not because you seriously think you two stand a chance in making another marriage work."

"Yeah," Candy said. By this time her throat was so tight from swallowing tears she could barely speak. "That sounds about right."

"So, see? That's why you have to go. It'll break

Kelly's heart if she thinks for a second her plan to reunite you two didn't work.''

''Well, we wouldn't want that, now, would we?'' After giving Mona another hug, Candy said, ''I better get going. I'm sure Jake's waiting.''

''But you *are* going Saturday night, right?''

''Oh, I'll be there all right,'' Candy said. What she didn't say was that instead of an evening gown, she might be wearing full armor and boxing gloves!

''YOU'RE AWFULLY QUIET,'' Jake said twenty minutes into their drive.

''Yup.''

''What're you thinking?''

''I doubt you'd want to know.''

''Try me,'' he said, casting his stupid sexy grin her way before turning his attention back to the road. His dark hair was all mussed and her fingertips itched from the memory of raking through it less than twenty-four hours earlier.

''Okay, why not? If anyone deserves to hear what's on my mind, it's you, you scum-sucking, sloth-toed, cross-eyed creep.'' So as not to wake Bonnie, Candy hurled her insults in a pleasant conversational tone.

''Excuse me?'' Jake said.

''You heard me.''

''Dammit.'' He tightened his grip on the wheel. ''Did Dietz say something to you?''

''No, but Mona sure did.''

''Oh, man…'' He plowed his right hand through his hair, mussing it all the more. ''I was afraid of something like this.'' Eyeing a scenic pull-off about a hundred yards down the road, he slowed, pulled the car over, then placed it in park before turning off the engine. "Okay, Candy. Let me have it. I deserve every insult you can think of and more."

She sighed. "That's the crazy part. I'm mad, all right. But as fed up as I am with you, I'm even more frustrated with myself."

"Why?"

She laughed. "Because truth be told, I knew exactly what you were up to. I just didn't want to believe it. Being with you again, laughing, reminiscing about old times, all of it just felt too darned good—too real—to have been set up."

He unfastened his seat belt and slid across the seat, pulling her into a fierce hug. "That's because it *was* real, Candy. Hell, I tried telling you about Dietz and Warren's reverse-psychology plan Tuesday night, but chickened out. And then, Wednesday morning, when Kelly hinted that you wanted me to stay just as bad as I wanted to stay, well…it seemed like fate was stepping in. So I let it. I'm sorry for ever including those guys in this mess but, Candy, you have to understand my level of desperation."

"I do," she said, hazarding a glance at Bonnie's angelic sleeping face. Her cheeks were flushed and a tiny spit bubble glistened at the corner of her cherry lips. "Especially after getting to know Bonnie. I mean, I thought I would be immune to her charms, but I'm not—not even a little bit. Yesterday, while we were out sailing, I even caught myself wondering if she was having a good time with Warren and Franny's kids, and if she'd gotten anything healthy to eat for lunch or was filling up on junk food. And last night, when I rocked her in your chair..." She clutched her chest, "My God, Jake, the feeling of bliss was tantamount to eating a dozen decadent chocolates. What do I do with that? What can I possibly do?"

"How about celebrate?"

"What? Are you crazy? Me being attached to a baby is hardly cause for celebration. This is *me* you're talking to, Jake. Candy—the woman who vowed to never, *ever* have a child."

"So? What if you renounced that vow?"

"I can't do that! I spent the last ten years adhering to that vow."

He groaned, washed his face with his hands. "Work with me, Candy. Because no matter how hard I try, I just can't see the point in you keeping a vow that makes you miserable."

"Because I *have* to. It's not a choice, Jake. I thought you knew that?"

"And I thought we've been all over this? This curse you think you have, it's all up here." He tapped his index finger to her temple. "Meanwhile, the *real* you is down here, just bursting to get out." He now pressed that dangerous roving hand of his against her chest and his heat, his hope, seeped through her, weaving its way into her soul.

She wanted to believe he was right. Oh, how she wanted to believe. But could she?

Chapter Eleven

Slanted sunbeams transformed the towering hardwood forest into a cathedral, resplendent in daisies and dogwoods and elegantly fading red buds. A pair of robins sang, a tree frog chirped. A soft breeze rustled new leaves and Bonnie's blond tufts. Candy smoothed them down, pressing a quick kiss to the sleeping angel's forehead.

"Want me to carry her?" Jake asked.

Candy shook her head. "This sling bears her weight pretty well." *Besides which,* she admitted only in her heart, *cradling her this close feels indescribably good—like a miracle. A miracle I never dared pray for, yet somehow quietly, wonderfully came true.*

"You two look good together," Jake said, stopping a few feet ahead on the trail.

"Thanks."

"You're welcome."

"This spot look familiar?" At the fork in the trail, one route led up, the other down toward a daisy-strewn embankment. A creek gurgled among topsy-turvy boulders that resembled a giant's game of marbles.

One boulder in particular caught Candy's eye. It towered beside the creek, its sloping top carpeted in luminescent moss.

Pulse surging at a suddenly erratic beat, she licked her lips.

This was the place. The place where the girl she used to be—the girl so full of hope for a glorious future—lay for hours, drunk on sunshine and her new husband's powerful spell.

He held out his hand to her. "Come on," he said. Interlocking her fingers with his, she realized his tender expression told her all she needed to know.

He remembers, too.

"Wh-why did you bring me here, Jake?"

"Why do you think?"

Right hand still holding hers, he brushed his left against the crown of her head, smoothing her hair.

"I truly don't know. If I did, I wouldn't have asked."

He sighed, looked to their rock, then back to her. "In this place, more than any other, I felt like we connected. We shared what really mattered," he said. "And I want us to do that again."

"So I'll agree to marry you?"

"I'd be lying if I said that wasn't true. But even more than that," he said, cradling her face with both of his big, warm hands, "I want what we used to have, Candy, back before I ever even mentioned the word 'kid.' Don't you see? I want *you*. I want my best friend back."

Tears welled in the corners of Candy's eyes and she swallowed hard trying to fight them back. She didn't want to cry—not now, when for once, life looked so good.

With the pads of his thumbs, he brushed away her tears, kissed the corners of each of her eyes before murmuring his lips against hers. She tasted her own salty tears, and for an instant, warning bells pealed in her heart.

Don't do this, Candy! Don't fall for him again— he'll only bring you pain!

What about your vows?

You know you'll make a lousy mom and wife.

Tell Jake to leave. To take his spellbindingly beautiful baby with him. It's the only way. The only way you'll ever be guaranteed a life free of pain. Granted, it'd also be a life void of delirious highs, but then who needs or even wants those when faced with the possibility of also having the inevitable devastating lows surely to come.

On the verge of asking Jake to take her home, Candy fought for air.

All of Jake's talk about her fears of inheriting her mother's inadequacies being unfounded was just that. Talk.

But then Bonnie stirred against her, sweetly resting her cheek against Candy's afraid-to-trust heart, and then a curious thing happened.

Like a butterfly emerging from its cocoon, old fears sloughed away and out came hope—an emotion so far removed from Candy's vocabulary she'd forgotten such a thing even existed.

"Jake?" she asked, her voice barely carrying above the gurgling stream.

"Yes?"

"I need you to be dead honest. What you said the other night, about you thinking I'd make a good mom. Did you mean it, or was that just a line?"

"I can't believe after all we've shared the past few days, that you even have to ask."

"Yeah, well…" A strangled laugh escaped Candy's lips. "It's kind of something I need to know. And seeing how you did start this week off by trying to manipulate me via Dietz's lamebrained plan, even you have to admit that you having said all those nice things just to woo me into your camp isn't entirely out of the realm of possibility."

"No, it's not," he said, washing his fingers up and down her forearms. "But here's the deal." He hardened his jaw, fixed her with a serious stare. "The only time I've *ever* lied to you was earlier this week, when I said I was leaving. Yeah, I had thoughts of just taking off. But truthfully, I knew I'd never leave Lonesome without you—for if I did, that meant losing Bonnie, which is something I'm not prepared— Hell, something I'm not even capable of doing."

"Right, which only gives you all the more incentive to lie."

"True. But that's just it—I came here prepared to lie, cheat and steal my way back into your good graces. But the funny thing is, after five minutes of being with you, my plans went out the window. That's when I realized my being here, back in Lonesome, back with you, wasn't just about keeping Bonnie. But about keeping me.'' Jake paused for a breath, looked to the stream.

Man, this was hard.

He'd come here today thinking they would have a nice picnic lunch. Steal a few more kisses. Never did he think he'd end up on the hot seat.

''Confession time,'' he said. ''I never really got over losing you, Candy. And the truth is, I need that closure. Even though I don't want to get on with my life, I have to. It's time. For my sake, for Bonnie's.''

''Then what are you doing here with me, when you know our long-term goals are diametrically opposed?''

''We're not talking long-term—only a year. If, in that year, we've regained our friendship, what can the harm be? I mean, who knows how we might feel.''

''About each other?''

''Sure. I suppose, but really, I'm thinking about life in general.'' *Each other.* Wow, how many times had he wanted to believe if only Candy would genuinely talk to him, open herself up, that they might once again be a couple?

Too many times to count. But that kind of thinking had been a long time ago.

He was older now—and he hoped wiser. He no longer believed in happily-ever-afters, but he sure as hell believed in living every breath in the moment. And at that moment, he wanted his breaths mingling with Candy's!

Hugging her to him, the child he desperately loved between them, Jake said, ''Look, I can't make any promises. I can't promise if you marry me, that you won't undergo some freak Jekyll/Hyde transformation. All I can do is promise that if such a thing should happen, I'll be right here…ready to help with silver crosses, garlic, wooden stakes—the works.''

"Jake?" Candy all but shrieked, pushing herself out of his arms. "You think it might come to that? That I'll be like some kind of vampire you'll have to ax in the middle of the night? I thought you said my fears are all in my head?''

"They are," he said, cinching her back into his arms. "Which is why I'm able to joke about them now.''

"Oh." She sucked her lower lip between her teeth for a quick nibble.

Tucking his hand beneath her chin, he said, "That's right, *oh*. I trust you, Candy. If I didn't, do you think we'd even be having this conversation?''

A SIMPLE LUNCH of a ham sandwich, chips and grape pop filling her tummy, Candy reclined on the moss-covered boulder, not only drinking in the warm sun, but also the sights and sounds of Bonnie's giggles.

She and her daddy were inspecting a roly-poly, and every time the poor bug curled into a ball, the infant laughed.

Candy hadn't realized the baby could so tightly focus her attention, but then she guessed there were a lot of new things she'd learned this week—chief among them being the surprise of how tightly she'd focused her own attentions on Bonnie.

Just think, four days earlier, Candy's biggest worry had been missing one of the connecting flights on her trip to Peru. Now, since discovering even the wildest adventure travel seemed tame in comparison to the thrills she got every time she so much as looked at Bonnie or Jake, she rarely even thought of her trip.

What did that mean?

"You're awfully quiet over there," Jake said.

"Mmm, sorry." She let out a yawn, followed by a lazy stretch.

"There's nothing to be sorry about. One of the things I've missed most about being with you is little things like not feeling I have to fill every second with small talk."

"Swell," she said, flashing him a grin. "Am I supposed to take that as a compliment? That the thing you find most compelling about me is my lack of conversation?"

Plucking the head from a dandelion, he flung it at her, but she darted just in time for it to land safely on the stream, then begin its float toward Lonesome Lake.

Laughing, Candy wagged her tongue at him before teasing, "Missed me, missed me, now you gotta kiss me."

"That how it works?"

Ignoring the perilous speed of her pulse, she didn't just meet his dark gaze but allowed herself the pleasure of drowning in it. Twirling a lock of hair, she said, "The rhyme clearly spells out the rules."

"That it does."

"So what are you going to do about it?"

He pushed aside the bag of corn chips resting between them to scoot a foot closer.

Nestled into a natural hollow in the rock, Bonnie contentedly sucked her toes.

Inches away, Jake said, ''What do you want me to do about it?''

''You're working very hard to make this difficult for me, aren't you?''

''Why, whatever do you mean, Mrs. Peterson?''

''Ms. Jacobs.''

''Right. Sorry, I keep forgetting.'' He scooted closer still, making Candy's humming body all but cry out with long-forgotten needs. Needs that until Jake had awakened them at the boathouse, and again on that remote beach, she'd been quite content in pretending she'd never even wanted, let alone needed like her next breath! Once again having him so near, yet so far, she was no longer able to play her game of pretending those needs weren't there.

Truth was, she *did* need him. Want him.

She wanted him, and his baby girl, and the giddy joy just being with them brought to her normally dull existence. She wanted to make new candies, naming them in Bonnie's honor. She wanted to launch new projects on the house. The ones she'd been too stubborn to admit to not being able to complete without a man's help—without Jake's help—for in his presence, no other men existed.

''Lie flat for me,'' he said, his voice a throaty caress.

''What?''

''You heard me.''

''Why? What're you going to do?''

''Have mind sex.''

"This is a joke, right?"

He shook his devilishly handsome head.

"Why here? Why now?"

"Why not? I've never seen you look more beautiful. Your hair all loose about your shoulders. All of that exposed skin of yours glowing with sweat. Hell, if the munchkin weren't here, just like I did almost ten years ago on this very spot, I'd ease you onto your back. Push up the hem of that blouse of yours, giving the sun a nice view of your perfectly rounded belly…"

Candy swallowed hard. *I remember. Oh, Lord, how I remember.* "Then what?"

"Seems to me, I undid the button on those skimpy jean cutoffs you used to tease me with. Those things hugged your sweet behind like paint. And it made me jealous. Jealous as hell of a pair of shorts. Wanna know why?"

She nodded.

"Because back then, you used to be mine. And no one, or thing, had a right to touch any of your curves but me."

"And now?"

He laughed, cast her a sexy-slow wink. "Now…I'm thinking with all your traipsing around the house wearing nothing but that scrap of a cat pajama top and your panties, and then today, wearing that supposedly innocent white blouse, you just might be leading me back down the road to ruin."

"What's wrong with my blouse?" she asked, toying with satin ribbon drawstrings dangling from the low-cut gathered bodice.

"Nothing, assuming you're a man who likes temptation. I mean, sitting close to you like I am, all I'd have to do to sneak a peek at those luscious breasts of yours would be this..." He reached for another dandelion, then slid it down the front of her blouse, using it as a gentle wedge to better his view.

Candy's heart raced when he leaned closer still, close enough to press his lips to the pliant swell spilling over the lacy cups of her bra.

Her nipples instantly hardened and she groaned, raking her fingers through the hair on the back of his head, urging him still closer.

She arched her head back and he switched course, pressing kisses to her chest, her collarbone, her throat, before finally, blessedly, her lips.

In a dizzying spiral he shifted her on top of him, and in that exquisite instant there could be no doubt as to how much he wanted her.

How much she wanted him.

He deepened his kiss, stroking her tongue with his, sweeping one hand beneath the fall of her hair, sliding the other into the back pocket of her shorts. "Damn, this sweet behind of yours..." he said on a ragged groan. "Gets me every time."

"Complaining?" she asked, breathing hard from an exhilarating lack of air.

"Not on your life."

"Great. Then I've got a suggestion."

He raised his eyebrows. "Let me guess, you want me to carry you to the next rock over so we'll have more privacy?"

"No," she said, giving him a little swat.

"Then what?"

"What I want is for you to take me back to the house, then for once make love to me in a proper setting."

"Oh, I get it. You wanna do it on the kitchen table."

For that, he got another swat. "Ever heard of a bed?"

Blasting her with his sexy-slowest grin, he shook his head. "Beds are for wimps. If you don't like the sound of the table, we'll just take this show to the hall stairs."

AS IT TURNED OUT, after playing peekaboo with Bonnie all the way home, then feeding her, bathing her, diapering and dressing her, playing with her, feeding her, reading to her, changing her diaper, changing her clothes again, then still finding her eyes wide open, by nine o' clock Friday night, Jake slumped in one recliner, Candy in the other. Both were too tired to move, let alone make love, even in a tame place like the bed.

As for Jake's earlier plans to take Candy on the stairs or kitchen table, he figured that'd just have to wait until he could once again walk.

On her fuzzy pink blanket in front of the TV, Princess Bonnie gummed a plastic block.

Along with the electronics, Jake had bought an assortment of DVDs. Disney's *Beauty and the Beast* was playing and while he'd never admit it, he was getting far more choked up by the ending than his kid.

"Think she'll ever sleep?" Candy asked. Even with her eyes shut, hair in glorious disarray, baby drool, peaches and spaghetti sauce dribbled on her once-white blouse, he couldn't remember ever seeing her look more pretty.

Course, he vaguely remembered having that same thought earlier in the woods, but now…now she looked like so much more than just his sexy dream woman.

Now, she looked like his baby's mom.

Damn, what a turn-on.

"No," Jake said, shifting his fly that'd suddenly grown a few sizes too small. "I don't think she'll ever close her eyes. Someday, she'll flit off to college and paramedics will just find me, old and gray, sitting in some recliner, still waiting for her to fall asleep."

When Candy laughed, Jake said, "You think I'm kidding, but just wait, it'll happen, and—hey, where did you find the energy to laugh? I'm jealous."

Scrunching onto her side to see him better, Candy said, "Funny, but tired as I am, I feel this strange sort of energy, too."

"If you say so."

She tossed a throw pillow at him, but missed.

"Missed me, missed me, now you gotta kiss me."

"You didn't kiss me."

"Did, too. It might have taken me a while to get warmed up, but in the end, you got what you wanted. I know your game. All you women are the same, just using poor, defenseless guys like me for sex."

"Oh," Candy said through a laughing splutter.

"And at the moment, you really look up to servicing me."

"That a challenge?" Jake asked, a naughty twinkle in his velvety-brown gaze.

"Maybe." Candy turned her attention back to the movie. It was almost over and the Beast was transforming himself in a myriad of slight yet enchanting ways. In a strange sense, she felt the story paralleled her own week-long journey.

At the start she'd been firmly convinced nothing Jake could ever do or say would convince her to marry him. But now…now, she was thinking he was right. About her fears over being a bad mom being just as unfounded as her assumption that she'd be a bad wife.

Who knew what the future might bring?

And tonight, who cared? Because she was daring to think that maybe, just maybe, everything she'd ever wanted or needed was right here in this room.

"You're quiet again," Jake said. "Thinking about how hot a time we're going to have doing it on top of the washer?"

"Jake! Honestly, don't you think about anything but *you know what?*"

His expression turned serious. "Now that you mention it, I've been doing an awful lot of thinking about tomorrow." He straightened in his chair, pulled in the recliner's footrest and rested his elbows on his knees. "I don't know about you, but for me this past week has been like an island in the storm. I've lived in the moment, just assuming everything would all work out, but now…"

"You're worried about my answer at the reunion tomorrow night?"

He nodded.

"Look," she said, straightening her recliner, too. "It wouldn't be fair of me to get your hopes up by hinting one way or the other at my decision. I mean, one minute I think I want nothing more than to once again be your wife. The next, my old doubts and fears start in again with their incessant nagging. Those fears are a part of me, and as much as I'd like them to leave me alone, it isn't that easy. No matter how hard I wish, they won't just magically go away."

"I know," he said. "Which is why I'm not going to pressure you. Even if you decide to stick with your trip to Peru. I'll understand."

"Will you, Jake?"

"Truthfully, it might take a while. But yeah. We've made a lot of progress this week on our friendship, and no matter what, as a friend, while I might not like your decision, I'll be honor bound to respect it—not to mention, you."

"Thank you," she said, tears welling.

"Hey, now, don't start that." Out of his chair, he went to her, pulling her up and into his arms. "No crocodile tears allowed during family fun night."

After sniffling she asked, "Not even if they're happy tears?"

"What would you be so happy about that it brings you to tears?"

"You, Jake. And the fact that after all this time, all the baggage between us, you're still such a good friend."

"Does that mean you're ready to try out the washing machine?"

"You wish," she said, rolling her eyes. "Bonnie doesn't take her chaperone duties lightly."

Jake glanced over his shoulder. "Oh, yeah? Take a look at that." Mr. Sandman had finally claimed Princess Bonnie who was now sound asleep on her tummy, knees drawn up, pink ruffled rump in the air.

"She's beautiful," Candy said, crossing the room to gently scoop her into her arms. "Come on. Come with me to tuck her in."

"Then do I get to tuck you in?" Jake asked with a rogue's wink.

Candy winked right back. "Tell you what, I'll at least promise to take your question under advisement."

Chapter Twelve

"Mommy, please... Please, Mommy, don't..."

Jake stirred, awakened by Candy's cries.

Obviously she was having one hell of a dream. Should he wake her?

Heck, yeah.

"Candy," he said, giving her a light shake. "Hey, Candy Cane, wake up. It's okay. It's only a dream."

She was slow returning to consciousness. Even then, in the moonlight washing the room, Jake could clearly see the pain and even the fear shining in her big, tear-dampened eyes.

Brushing the hair back from her forehead, she said, "Wow...I haven't had that dream in years."

"I take it it had something to do with your mother?"

"How'd you know?"

"You cried out for her."

"I did?" Candy pulled the sheet over her naked breasts, gazing out the picture window with its panoramic view of the diamond-strewn lake.

"Yeah, you did...which is making me think this

whole becoming even a temporary mom issue is more than you can handle.''

When she didn't reply, Jake tentatively reached out to her, smoothing his hand down her impossibly soft hair.

''I'm sorry,'' he said. And at that moment, he was. Profoundly. Swallowing hard, he said, ''You have to know…as much as I want to keep Bonnie, I never wanted to do it at your expense.''

''I know,'' she said, still focusing her gaze out the window instead of on him.

''If you know, then why won't you at least look at me?''

''Because the dream wasn't about you, okay?'' This time she did turn to him, blasting him with hollow-eyed pain that if he lived to be a hundred and twenty he'd never forget. ''It was about me. It was a reminder of just how bad my mother really was.''

''Tell me about it,'' Jake urged. ''I always used to feel better when I shared my nightmares with Mom or Dad.''

Candy flashed him a fragile smile. ''That's just it, this wasn't a nightmare, but my everyday life, and my mom was hardly the kind of woman I'd snuggle with when I was scared.'' Gazing back toward the window, she sighed. ''This dream was about when I had stomach flu. I'm not sure how old I was—maybe seven or eight. Anyway, it was a Saturday, and Daddy was out of town at some Lion's Club thing. Mom was dressing to go to Springfield with one of her friends. I was supposed to have had a sitter, but at the last minute, she called to cancel, so Mom told me to be a big girl and baby-sit myself. Right before she walked out the door, I begged her not to leave, crying that I thought I might be sick. She accused me of lying just to keep her home. But then I threw up— all over her best powder-blue suit. It was horrible. Puke everywhere.''

Pulling her knees to her chest, Candy hugged them, swallowed hard. "She slapped me. She said, 'Don't you *ever* do that again.' I remember just lying there on the entry hall floor. Shivering. Wet from my own vomit. She stripped in front of me, throwing her clothes to the floor and kicking her powder-blue pumps across the room.''

Shaking her head, Candy said, "I'll never forget the noise those shoes made clacking against first the plaster wall, then down to the hardwood floor. Without giving me a second glance, Mom headed for the bathroom. The shower went on and, I don't know, maybe thirty minutes later, she left out the back door. Didn't come home until Sunday afternoon.''

Jake pulled Candy into his arms, hugging her fiercely. "What did your dad say?''

"He never knew.''

"Why, Candy?" Pulling back, he cradled her dear, beautiful face in his hands, brushing a stray tear with the pad of his thumb. "Why didn't you ever tell him? Or your grandfather? Or even a teacher or Kelly?''

She shrugged. "That was normal to me. I guess until I got a little older, I didn't know what a good mom was supposed to be like. And then…well, by then, she'd convinced me that everything bad she dished out, I had coming. I was a bad girl.''

"But you weren't," Jake said. "You must know that by now?"

She nodded. "Sure. I've seen all the talk shows on abusive parents, read all the books. In my head I know none of what she did was my fault, but inside…" She took a shuddering deep breath. "Really believing I wasn't somehow to blame. That's the tough part. That's the part I'm terrified of grappling with every day for the rest of my life."

"Have you thought about seeing a counselor?"

"I did. Right after Grandpa died, I felt like I needed to talk some things out, so I saw a woman in Springfield. She was the one who suggested I distance myself from my past. So, see? My trip is like a prescription for my soul."

Jake groaned and raked his fingers through his hair. "I'm no expert, but do you think traveling halfway around the world is what she really meant?"

"What else would she have meant?"

"I don't know. Maybe more along the lines of what I was saying just the other day. That maybe instead of dwelling on your past family, you might want to think about starting a new family."

"Undoubtedly with you?"

He grinned. "Who else?"

LONG AFTER Jake succumbed to sleep, holding Candy's backside snug against him, she lay awake, staring at the ceiling, smoothing her hand along the top of his.

Never had she wished more for an easy answer. A crystal-ball glimpse into her future. If she married

Jake, what would become of her? Would she turn out just like her mom, or could Candy write a new script for the rest of her life?

Closing her eyes, she saw herself standing beside Jake, helping Bonnie take her first steps, ride her first bike, learn to swim. She saw them laughing over simple family dinners, hosting lazy Sunday-afternoon cookouts and giggling slumber parties.

Even better, Candy saw herself never again being lonely, but surrounded by not just the love of her husband and adopted daughter, but the love of still more children. The children she'd denied Jake, even though secretly wanting more than he ever could have imagined.

All she had to do was say yes to Jake at the reunion tomorrow night, and all of those dreams and so many more would be well on their way to coming true. All she had to do was dare to hope, and she held the key to opening that wondrous door to bliss.

Yes, but what about other doors…the ones that lead to living a life like your mother's?

Heart pounding, Candy leaned closer to Jake.

No.

Never again would she believe herself capable of becoming her mother. Jake was right. That fear lived only in her head. Her current actions were the real proof of her future intentions.

Right.

Current actions that include being incapable of making a decision one way or the other.

What if, just like you did, Bonnie one day falls ill. What if you can't decide whether or not to take her to the doctor? What if you decide to handle her fever on your own but it soars out of control? Then what are you gonna, do, huh? What's Jake going to say when his precious baby ends up in the hospital by the hands of a woman like you? A woman who has no business being a mother.

"MORNING," Jake said, planting a kiss on first Bonnie's cheek then Candy's. "You two are up awfully early."

From where she stood at the kitchen counter, holding Bonnie on her hip with one arm and stirring biscuit dough with the other, Candy shrugged. "I figured it was either get up early enough to beat you to the skillet or suffer through another day of indigestion."

He clutched his chest. "That hurts, Candy Cane— even worse than my chili omelet heartburn. So?" he asked, pulling out a chair at the table. "What's on the agenda for today? More hiking? Hang around here and watch movies while eating an obscene amount of junk food?"

"Actually," Candy said, plonking her dough out of the bowl and onto a marble baking board, "I thought we might spend today apart. Here, would you mind holding the princess while I roll out the dough?" She gestured for Jake to come get Bonnie— which he did.

Back in his chair, nuzzling the baby's fluffy blond hair, he asked, "What changed?"

"Excuse me?"

Jake slipped Bonnie into her high chair, handed her a napkin and spoon to play with, then stormed over to Candy. Hands around her waist, he turned her to face him. "You heard me. But just so we get things clear, specifically I'm asking what's changed since we made love last night and now?"

"Nothing, Jake. Please, let me get breakfast done."

"I don't give a damn about breakfast. What I do care about is you, Candy. Does this have something to do with that bad dream?"

She sharply looked away.

"That's it, isn't it? You have one dream about your deadbeat mom and suddenly your irrational fears about somehow becoming her take precedence over what's real? Explain that for me, Candy. Explain that to Bonnie."

She twirled a lock of hair, in the process, dusting herself with flour. Even with a streak of white hair, Jake had never seen her look more beautiful. But, dammit, she'd brought him to the end of his rope. He couldn't make her talk any more than he could make her marry him.

Turning away, he said, "Give me a few minutes to get some pureed peaches down the munchkin, and then we'll head out."

"Oh, Jake," she said, her voice hoarse. "Please don't leave. Not like this."

"No. It's not a problem. I'll pack up and be gone in thirty minutes."

"I didn't mean for you to *leave* leave. I meant that we should spend today by ourselves. You know, thinking, before tonight."

"What's the point? You're just going to turn me down."

"You don't know that!"

"Yeah," he said with a snort. "But obviously, you do."

He slipped Bonnie from her chair, cradling her close. "Come on, kiddo, let's go see what Dietz is having for breakfast."

"I THOUGHT YOU might be here." Kelly flashed Candy a wave before pulling up a tall stool at Candy Kisses' ice-cream counter.

"Want your usual?" Candy asked, already reaching for a waxed paper cup.

Kelly shook her head.

Aside from the jangle of Kelly setting her keys to the marble counter and the muted laughter coming from a pair of young moms and their babies seated at a back table, the shop was quiet. Had been all day.

Kelly said, "I ran into Jake and Bonnie."

"Oh?" Candy wiped a sudsy rag across the already-clean counter.

"They were feeding the ducks over at the city pond. A new batch of baby geese just hatched and Bonnie got a kick out of watching them bobble around."

"That's nice. What were you doing at the park?"

"Painting. That big weeping willow by the swan house was this week's assignment for my watercolor class."

Candy scrubbed harder.

Bonnie surrounded by baby geese. Could there be any cuter sight?

"Jake asked about you."

"Anything he wanted to know, he could've asked me."

"Not this."

Candy froze. "Look, you've beaten the bush to death. Whatever you came to say, spit it out."

"Jeez, bite my head off." Kelly glanced at the smiling faces at the back table.

"Sorry. I didn't get much sleep."

"Whatever. All I wanted to say is that Wednesday night, Jake called. He wanted to know if finding your mother, talking to her, telling her how you feel might change how you feel about—well, you know…"

"Having kids?"

"Yeah."

"So? What'd you tell him?"

"For the record, I told him not to look for your mom. But you know, now that I've had a chance to think about it, maybe it'd be a good idea for you to vent your frustrations on the woman who—"

"Oh, great," Candy said, back to scrubbing. "So I suppose I can now look forward to a family reunion?"

Kelly sighed. "No. If you'd let me finish, you would know I told Jake as healthy as I think such a conversation would be, that I also think whether or not you choose to have it is a decision only you can make."

"You said that?"

Tears in her eyes, Kelly nodded.

"So why, if you did the right thing, do you look like you're about to cry?"

"Candy, I—"

The bell above the door jingled.

In strolled Jake.

Just the sight of him lurched Candy's heart. His chiseled jaw, strong forehead, dark-as-sin eyes. How it had happened, she didn't know, but despite her best efforts to the contrary, in that exquisite moment, she knew she hadn't just fallen for him again. She'd fallen in love with him.

Love!

"Where's Bonnie?" Candy asked, scrubbing her way through the counter to China.

"She's hanging out with Warren and Franny's kids. They've got some teenager coming over to sit tonight and they asked if I wanted her to watch Bonnie, too."

"It was nice of them to think of us needing a sitter." *Us.* She'd actually referred to her and Jake as an us!

"Yeah, I thought so, too." He glared at Kelly.

She glared back before saying, "Well, I'd better be going. With the big night just hours away, I should get busy."

"Sure," Candy said. "See you later." Was it just her, or was the tension between Kelly and Jake thicker than two-week-old taffy?

Just as Kelly was almost to the door, Candy called, "Wait!"

"What?" Kelly asked.

Candy hustled out from behind the counter. "Before Jake came in, you were about to tell me something."

"It's no big deal," Kelly said, hand on the door, body angled to bolt.

"Obviously it was a big deal, or you wouldn't have had tears in your eyes. What's up, Kel?"

"Really, nothing. Besides, Jake should be the one to tell you." Kelly squeezed her in a fierce hug, then hustled out the door.

"That was weird," Candy said. "Do you have any idea what she's talking about?"

"I could sure go for one of your Coco Locos."

"I'll get you a dozen just as soon as you tell me what's going on."

"Not here, baby." He took her right hand in his. Gave it a squeeze. "Trust me on this."

Heart pounding, she said, "Oh, my gosh, something's happened to Bonnie. Is it something to do with that Elizabeth Mannford woman? Did she come for her? Is that it? Has she taken Bonnie back to Florida?"

"No," Jake said, smoothing fallen hair back from her brows. He flashed her a weak smile. "But I'm touched that you care."

"Of course, I care. I—" It had been on the tip of her tongue to admit that she loved Bonnie, every bit as much as she loved him. It had been on the tip of her tongue to tell him right then and there that not only did she love him but that she wanted to marry him, to have his babies and everything that that entailed…when she noticed the odd intensity of his gaze. His normally tanned complexion turned pale and his grin slowly faded to a definite frown.

"Jake?" she said. "Come on, you're scaring me."

"Thank you!" The petite blonde dressed in head-to-toe matching mother/baby Gap wear waved on her way out the door. Her friend followed suit.

"You're welcome," Candy said with a friendly wave. "Come back soon."

"We will!"

"There," she said to Jake once the foursome strolled out the door. "Happy now? They're gone." Sudsy rag in hand, she headed to their table to clear the dishes and wipe it down. "Come on, already. Spill it."

He cleared his throat, joined her beside the table. "Sit down."

"I don't want to sit. I've got too many things to do."

"*Sit.*" Something in his tone told her to just this once do as he asked. Plopping her rag on the table, she pulled out one of the twisted iron chairs and fell into it. "There. I'm sitting."

He sat, too. "I did something the other day, before we'd gotten so close, that I think you're not going to be happy about."

Candy put her fingers to his lips. "Shh, not another word. Kelly already told me about how you wanted to find my mother, but that she told you no. The thought was incredibly sweet. I'm not even a teensy bit upset with you for coming up with the idea."

"But, Candy, I—"

"Really, Jake. It's okay. It's funny, on Monday, I never would have thought there was a chance of me finding peace with my mom. But now—" she shrugged "—I don't want to see her. Who knows?

Maybe just thinking this much about her has flicked a switch in my mind. I started off today hating her. That dream I had last night brought so many unpleasant memories crashing back. But then, working here, among so many happy people, I realized that maybe like the counselor said, it's time I distance myself from the past. It's time I take responsibility for my own happiness. Not look for it in family or friends or even exotic places, but just like you said, look here…Inside.'' Taking his hand in hers, she pressed it to her chest.

"Oh, Candy," he said, eyes welling with tears. "God, I don't want to tell you this."

"Jake, I just told you I know about your wanting to find my mom. I know, and I don't care. I mean, I care but—''

"Stop." A nerve ticked in his jaw. "Being the jerk I am, I didn't take Kelly's advice. I went ahead and called a private detective friend in Palm Breeze."

Hands to her mouth, Candy shook her head. "No, Jake. Please tell me you didn't…''

"Believe me, no one wishes that more than me, but yeah," he said with a sharp laugh. "I did have my friend look for her. I'd forgotten all about it, then this morning, on my cell phone, my friend gave me a call. He found your mom. I'm sorry. So sorry. But your mom…Candy, she's—''

"You don't mean…'' Candy vehemently shook her head.

This isn't happening. Can't be happening.

"Yes, Candy. I'm sorry. Your mother's dead.''

Chapter Thirteen

Jake crept open the door to Candy's bedroom to find her still asleep. Golden late-afternoon sun streamed through a crack in the shades, illuminating her cheek and strands of fiery red in her sable hair.

He felt lower than low for not only being the bearer of her bad news, but for being the one who'd uncovered it.

At first she'd been spooky-calm, efficiently calling the teens who were supposed to watch the shop that night and asking them to come in early.

Within fifteen minutes, help had arrived.

Jake had offered to drive Candy home, planning to return later for her van, but she'd stoically refused. Only after she'd pulled into the drive, placed her van in park, then turned off the engine, did she break down.

She'd cried so hard that he'd carried her inside.

He held her on the sofa, prepared her a steaming bath and held her more there.

Finally, around three, exhaustion claimed her and

he helped her dry off and dress, then tucked her into bed.

While he hated the very idea of leaving, he had an errand to run. One that couldn't be delayed a minute longer if his evening was to unfold as planned.

Though he hadn't yet spoken with Candy about it, he assumed in light of the news he'd just handed her, they wouldn't be going to the reunion. But if he had anything to say about it, they'd sure as hell still have a special night.

As for what happened after that…

Who knew?

Since returning to Lonesome, to the woman he used to call his wife, there were times he'd doubted knowing his own name. He was so damned attracted to Candy. Most times, he wanted to hold her close and to never let go, but deep inside, he knew that even if by some miracle she agreed to temporarily marry him, that was just it. Their marriage would be a purely temporary thing.

In the past, he'd been hurt far too badly by her to ever even think about forming another long-term commitment.

Thankfully, Candy was giving off the same vibes— that they were having fun, but it was a fun never meant to last.

CANDY WOKE SLOWLY, as if stepping through a fog.

Thirsty. She was incredibly thirsty. And her eyes burned scratchy and dry.

I'm sorry. Your mother's dead.

The news hit her again, as did the fact that she'd died nearly twelve years earlier from lung cancer.

"Jake?" *Where are you? I need you.*

Darting her gaze across the shadowy room, she saw that he wasn't there. And more than anyone in the whole world, she missed him. Wanted him.

He'd been there all afternoon, though, holding her, rocking her, soothing her as the mother she mourned never had.

From the hall came a creak, then, "Hey, sleeping beauty. You're up."

"Sort of," she said, tucking her hair behind her ears. Glancing at her bedside clock, she said, "Wow, already after six, huh? Guess I better start getting ready. Judging by how rotten I feel, it's going to take me a while to look even halfway presentable."

"You can't be serious?" Jake said, frowning to see her slide out of bed. "There's no way I'm letting you near that reunion."

"You're not *letting* me?" Raising an eyebrow at his domineering tone, she wrapped him in a hug and rested her cheek against the solid wall of his chest. "Thanks for worrying about me, but really, Jake, I'm fine."

"You can't be. My mom died years ago and I'm still not fine."

"Yeah, but you're forgetting one very important thing," she said, releasing him to head for the closet. "In my mind, Mom was already dead. Your news just made it official."

"Grief—it's not that simple."

"For me it is."

He turned her to face him. "No, Candy, it isn't." Standing on tiptoes, she pressed a soft kiss to his lips. "Yes, it is. I mean, this may sound heartless, but I'm not sad because she's gone, but because of how many years I've wasted expecting her return. Not in the physical sense—but inside of me. Now that she's gone—*truly* gone… Don't you see what that means? She's gone inside me, too. I'm free."

More importantly…we're free.

Until that moment Candy hadn't known what her answer would be to Jake's proposal. But now…now she knew she'd say yes.

Jake frowned, slashing his fingers through his hair. "I want to believe you, but this time you're the one spouting too easy solutions."

"Nobody said any of this was easy, but it's a start. A start to healing. A start to living. Both of which are things I've put off for way too long."

"Okay then…" He sighed before pulling her into his arms. "For the record, I want it said that you need more time for the news about your mom to sink in, but if this is the way you claim to feel, far be it from me to botch your life up with further interference."

"Thank you."

"You're welcome. Now, how about a few happy surprises?"

"Mmm, I like surprises," she said, molding herself to him, drinking in his warmth, his strength.

"I know," he said chucking her under her chin. "Which is why, if you'd care to accompany me downstairs, numerous surprises await the pleasure of your beautiful smile."

"JAKE, it's gorgeous! How can I ever thank you?" Candy held the gold lamé gown to her body, twirling 'round and 'round.

"How about trying it on? Oh—and don't forget these..." From the pocket of his tux jacket, he withdrew what at first glance appeared to be a fistful of glowing emeralds.

Candy gasped. "Oh, Jake. Oh, my gosh."

Bearing his sexiest grin, he nestled the three-tier waterfall of emeralds around her neck. The weight felt akin to him gliding his hand across her chest. "Mind lifting your hair, then turning around?"

"Sure. Of course." She shivered when his fingertips tickled the back of her neck. "All of this is amazing. The dress. The necklace. The way you look in that tux. The catered dinner—even the way you set the dining room table with Grandma's china. If you'd rather stay in tonight, I'll be fine with it."

"No," he said, stepping back to survey his work. "As gorgeous as you look, I want every man in town knowing you're mine."

"WITHOUT FURTHER ADO, the king and queen of Lonesome High's Class of 1987..." Everyone's favorite English teacher, Mrs. Griffon, had a tough time getting the envelope open. But once she finally did, her smile faded into the kind of frown she only wore when everyone in class flunked a pop quiz. "Oh, my. Well, this is certainly an unexpected development."

"Who is it?" Larry Neimowitz called from the crowd.

"Yeah, hurry up already!" Pete Hargrove echoed. "We ain't gettin' any younger!"

Mrs. Griffon glowered all the harder. "Correction—we *aren't* getting any younger. And without further ado, believe it or not—the king and queen of the Class of 1987 are Miss Kelly Foster and Mr. Landon Dietz."

A collective gasp rippled through the Lonesome Country Club's decked out ballroom. Then a hearty round of wolf whistles and applause.

"He rigged this," Kelly hissed in Candy's ear. "I just know that awful Dietz did something to rig this."

"Oh?" Candy said. "Like you were trying to rig it for me and Jake to win?"

"You knew?" Kelly frowned. "Wait a minute. You *knew*… Which means…oh, no, don't tell me my very best friend did this to me?"

A sparkle in her eyes, Candy nodded. Jake, close by her side, slid his arm around her waist and she happily leaned closer. "I might know something and then again I might not."

From the bandstand at the front of the room, Mrs. Griffon said, "Mr. Dietz, Miss Foster, please make your way to the podium so that I can crown you then send you onto the dance floor for that all-important royal dance."

Kelly groaned. "I'm going to get you for this, Jacobs."

"Correction," Candy whispered in her friend's ear. "That would be *Peterson.*"

Kelly squealed. "Oh, my gosh! Does that mean what I think it does?"

"Almost. Shh, I haven't told him yet. Now go on and get your crown."

"Okay," Kelly said, giving her a quick hug. "But don't think I'm going to forget this stunt anytime soon."

TWENTY MINUTES AFTER the coronation, Jake noticed Dietz and Kelly still clenched in a dimly lit corner of the dance floor. "I thought you said those two don't get along?" he asked his own hot date.

"They don't, which is why I guessed they'd make a perfect couple."

Jake nodded. Sometimes it was easier to agree with Candy than to try to figure her out. Such as the way she'd handled the news about her mom. It didn't make sense. But then, nothing much he did made sense these days, starting with how attached he was starting to feel to his ex-wife.

"Ready for an answer?" she asked, snuggling deeper into his hold.

"That depends," he said. "Am I going to like it?"

Tilting her glance to meet his, she said, "I hope so."

Could this be the time she accepted his proposal? Her wide grin made his heart double the song's beat. At this point, as many times as he'd gotten his hopes up only to have them stomped, beaten and drop-kicked out the door, he was almost afraid to do any more hoping.

"Come on," she said, taking him by hand to lead him off the dance floor and onto the moonlit patio.

The country club sat at the opposite end of Lonesome Lake to her house, and the nighttime view was every bit as poetic. A light breeze rippled the water's surface, doubling the amount of stars by strewing an extra set across the water. The decoration committee had strung the trees with white lights and floated dozens of flickering candles in the pool. The dewy night air smelled of mown putting greens and women's perfume and lingering smoke from the grilled steaks they'd had for dinner.

Jake let Candy lead him to a secluded corner where the only light besides the winking ones high in the trees came from the glowing aqua pool. The temperature hovered near balmy perfection, and while music and laughter still drifted from inside, the sounds were muted, making it easy for Jake to hear Candy's sigh.

Oh, God, here it comes. She's turning me down!

After they'd both taken seats on a wooden bench, she rested her head on his shoulder. "Have you ever seen a more perfect night for a party?"

"Uh, no." He put his hand to his chest. How much more suspense could his poor heart take?

"Me, either."

"Candy, I don't mean to rush you, but—"

"You feel like you've been waiting long enough?"

"That's about the size of it."

"Then without further ado," she said, mocking Mrs. Griffon's deep voice. "I think Mr. Jake Peterson's in need of an answer." She giggled before clearing her throat. "That was tough. Wonder how she talks like that all the time?"

"Must be the cigars."

"Right," she said with a wink. "Anyway, where were we?"

We were just studying the play of moonlight in your hair. Memorizing the funny little way you lick your lips before you speak, and especially the way that dress hugs your mouth-watering curves.

"Oh, yes. Your answer. First," she said, licking her lips again before twirling a lock of her hair. "As you well know, I've never been big on spontaneity. To tell you the truth, it scares me to death, but then in light of hearing about Mom's death, I got to thinking that all of us are gifted with only a short time here on earth."

"Yeah…" Would she think him rude if he urged her to hurry it up?

"Well, seeing how we do just have a limited time, that got me to thinking about what a super time I've had with you and Bonnie. In fact, I've had such a great time, that I decided my answer will be…yes."

"Yes?" Relief didn't begin to describe the calm flooding his system. *Yes! She said yes!*

"Yes!"

What he hoped were happy tears escaped the corners of her big brown eyes. Not for the first time that night, he was grateful for her slinky dress, not just because of the way it hugged her curves, but because of how easy it made the process of sliding her onto his lap.

Where he kissed her.

Oh, did he kiss her.

Hard, soft, and every way in between. Stroking her tongue with his, he savored her unique flavor, basked in her innate goodness. Her generosity. Her selfless postponement of her trip just to ensure that he and Bonnie never had to live a day apart—at least until the munchkin left for college. But hey, there were a lot of colleges near Palm Breeze. Maybe she'd be one of those kids who always stayed close to home.

"Thank you. Thank you. A thousand times, thank you," he said, kissing her lips, her nose, her cheeks and eyelids.

"Thank you," she said, the tinkling laugh he loved spilling past kiss-swollen lips.

"Why would you thank me? You're doing me the favor."

She gave him a little swat. "You're so silly. I'm thanking you in advance for all the wonderful years we have ahead of us. I mean, come on, you didn't seriously think I'd just marry you and be a mother to Bonnie for one measly year, did you? Now that you've spent the past week showing me how awesome our family is going to be, I never want the three of us to ever again be apart."

"But, Candy, I—" *I don't want a real marriage. I thought I'd made that point clear?*

"Just think," she said, tilting her head back, dreamily gazing at the stars. "We can have a huge wedding at the house. Maybe we can renew our vows on the boat dock, then set up the reception in different food stations all over the yard. I know this sounds like a lot of work to do in a short time, but we have loads of friends and I'm sure they won't mind pitching in to help. Tell you what, go ahead and call Bonnie's social worker and that nasty old Elizabeth Mannford, too. Maybe they'll both want to come?''

Jake's mouth turned to cotton. Surely he wasn't hearing Candy right? Surely she was suggesting a big wedding for the sole purpose of impressing Mrs. Starling for her report to the judge?

Once again flinging her slender arms about his neck, she squeezed him with extra oomph. ''Our first wedding was special, but now that we know how precious the love was that we almost lost, I want our second wedding—our last wedding—to be the most crazy romantic night this town has ever seen. Candles and champagne. Dancing and a dozen bridesmaids and a flower girl…Jake? Is something wrong?''

He slid her off of his lap. Paced the small brick-paved area in front of their bench.

''I've overwhelmed you, haven't I? I'm sorry. It's just that now that I've finally made up my mind to go ahead with not just the wedding, but our lives, I can't make us official fast enough.'' Bouncing up from her seat, she pressed her palms to his chest. ''Suddenly, more than anything in the world, I want to be Mrs. Jake Peterson. Oh—and of course I want to be Bonnie's mommy, as well.''

Jake eased her away, tucked his hands in the pant pockets of his tux. A muscle ticked in his jaw. ''You know, as nice as all of that sounds, Candy, we don't need anything near that elaborate. I was thinking a simple ceremony at the Palm Breeze courthouse would do. That way, at the end of the year, when you're ready to go your way and me and Bonnie ours, the split will be easier. No witnesses, you know.''

Fearing he might be the cause of more shimmering tears, he aimed his gaze toward the lake.

"But, Jake," she said, quietly stepping up behind him. "Didn't you understand a word of what I said? That's just it. I don't want a temporary marriage with you, I want the real deal. I want forever and all that that implies."

Never had he hurt this bad.

Not when he broke his leg back in seventh grade.

Not when he signed their final divorce papers.

"Look, Candy," Jake said, his voice foreign and tinny to his own ears. "I don't know how to tell you this. Hell, after your generous offer, the last thing I want to do is seem ungrateful, but see, the thing is—"

"Oh, God, Jake. What? What's wrong? If a week is too long to wait, we'll head to Palm Breeze first thing in the morning. We can always come back to hold a blowout reception once Bonnie's adoption is final."

"No, it's not that," he said. "Your, uh, wedding plan sounds real nice."

"Then what?" The look she gave him was so luminous, so trusting, he didn't begin to know where to start. Problem was, he had to. He had no choice.

Self-preservation was a mighty powerful thing. The last time they split up had nearly done him in. He hadn't known himself capable of experiencing that much love…and ultimately, that much pain. He couldn't risk going through that kind of pain ever again. He couldn't. If that meant losing custody of Bonnie… Well, he'd just have to find some way to make it up to her. To make her understand that if Daddy lost his heart, he'd also be losing his soul.

"Okay," he said. "Here's the deal. I want to marry you. Hell, I'd kill to marry you. But only for a year."

She shook her head, slowly twirled a lock of hair. "I don't understand what you're saying. I love you, Jake. You're not making sense."

"That's just it," he said, squeezing her small hand in his. "I don't love you—not that way. I did once, but never again. I'm sorry, Candy. Really, I am, but a year is all I can give you. I don't dare give anything more."

Candy's free hand itched from wanting to slap Jake's supposedly concerned smile right off of his face. "This whole week has been nothing but a game to you, hasn't it? Woo me with TVs and picnics and making love all night long. Every funny and sexy and romantic thing you've done, cruelly designed to wring out the answer you wanted."

"That's not true," he said, grasping her firmly by her upper arms. "I would never do something like that."

"Oh, yeah? Then what do you think you've been doing?"

"Getting reacquainted with an old friend."

She laughed. "News flash, Jake. Old *friends* don't get naked. And they sure as heck don't kiss in every room of the house."

"Look—" He released her to slash his fingers through his hair. "I said I was sorry, okay? What more do you want?"

"Nothing. Not a damned thing. Just go away. I wish I'd never even met you."

"Yeah, well, as impossible as it may seem, right now I'm wishing the same thing. You might think this is a line, too, but the truth of the matter is that when you divorced me, I wasn't sure I'd even live through the pain. I know it's not macho, or cool, for a guy to be that much in love, but I was. If I were to fall that deep with you again, then have you walk out on me—or even worse, have you send me packing. I don't know what I'd do."

"But, Jake, I wouldn't do that. I would *never* do that. I love you. I see that now. I've always loved you. I've just been too screwed up about my mom to see that love."

Now it was his turn to laugh. "That's easy enough for you to say, but how do I know you mean it? Only hours ago, I told you your mother died, and now, here you are claiming you're ready to live happily ever after? I don't think so."

"Candy? Jake?" Beaming, hand in hand with Dietz, Kelly tugged her newly crowned king across the patio. "You two have some happy news to finally share?"

Candy, arms hugging her aching chest, turned her back to her friend.

"Jake?" Dietz asked. "What happened, man? Candy turn you down?"

"Can it, Dietz."

Kelly slipped her arm around Candy's shoulders. "Is everything all right?"

She burst into tears. "Super-duper. Isn't it, Jake?"

While Candy dashed inside, Jake aimed for the golf course.

Kelly told Dietz, "I'll follow Candy. You follow the bum."

"How do you know Jake's at fault here?"

"Trust me, I know."

"Yeah, well, Candy was at fault the first time they broke up."

"Yeah, well, I promise, she's not now." With a groan and an exasperated shake of her head, she said, "Never mind. We'll dispense blame later. For now, just go after Jake."

Chapter Fourteen

From her seat on the black velvet ladies' room settee, Candy looked up to see Kelly burst through the gilded door. "Leave me alone, okay?"

"Not okay," Kelly said. "First, tell me what happened. Did you decide not to marry Jake, after all?"

"No. Can you believe it? He decided not to marry me."

"What?" Kelly jiggled her finger in her ear, checking to see if the thing was even working because surely she hadn't heard her friend right.

"When I told him I wanted to marry him not just for a year but forever, he spouted some nonsense about not loving me, and how b-because of our divorce, he couldn't trust me."

"That's stupid."

"That's what I said, but he w-wouldn't listen."

"So what're you going to do?"

Hardening her jaw, Candy said, "Go home and pack."

"Not for that crazy eco trip to Peru?"

"Of course to Peru. Where else would I go?"

''I had hoped to camp out on Jake's Palm Breeze doorstep.''

''Why would I do a whacked thing like that?''

''Because you love him?''

''Correction—*used* to love him. Now, I'd just as soon spit at him than look at him.''

''So BASICALLY what you're saying is that you'd just as soon spit at her than look her?''

From his seat on the back of a golf cart, Jake slanted Dietz a dirty look. ''Hell no, that's not what I'm saying.''

''Then what are you saying? Because frankly, I got a little lost back around the time you were explaining how you feel like you love her but you don't.''

Jake groaned. ''Maybe even I don't know what I mean. This whole thing—it's complicated.''

''No it's not. You came here looking for a temporary wife and you found one. Even better, you found one you could ultimately live happily ever after with. Do you have any idea how rare that is?'' Dietz snatched an old golf ball from a bucket and flung it as far as he could. ''You might not believe this, but my whole life, I've been looking for a woman to love. Yet here you've had love handed to you on a gold lamé, sexy-as-sin platter and you're throwing it— her—away.''

Jake rocketed from his seat, the force of his movement bucking the cart so hard, Dietz had to hold on. ''Don't you dare talk to me about throwing Candy away. She's the one who dumped me. All I'm doing is returning the favor.''

"Yeah," Dietz said. "But at what cost?"

WHEN CANDY RETURNED home, it was to an empty house.

Jake had left the furniture and TV, but the clothing, the diapers—the souls—were gone.

For the longest time she sat at the top of the stairs, elbows on her knees, chin cupped in her hands.

"Well, Mom," she said, her voice echoing off lonely walls. "Guess you had the last laugh, huh? You taught me a long time ago that there was no such thing as forever when it comes to love, and I guess despite my best efforts to prove you wrong, in the end, you were right."

Pushing herself to her feet, she made the short trip to the kitchen. What she needed was cookies and milk—that is, assuming Jake hadn't taken her Nutter Butter.

He hadn't. And when Candy had a stack of at least six fisted in one hand and a glass of milk in the other, she hiked her fancy gold dress up to her thighs, then sat cross-legged in Jake's favorite recliner.

She tried working the remotes to find some horrible slasher movie that suited her mood, but in the end, all she found was a tearjerking classic.

She'd hoped to at least wait for the movie's end to spill buckets of tears, but couldn't hold out that long. Setting her snack on a side table, Candy cupped her face in her hands and cried—not because of her mom or broken vows, but because of the irony of the fact that through Jake's help she'd finally come to see that her fears of becoming a bad wife and mom were just that—stupid, irrational fears.

She'd overcome so much in the past week, worked through so many issues on a speed track to emotional well-being, yet what had all that work gotten her?

Squat.

Seeing how Jake wouldn't marry her, she was no closer to having a family than she'd been on Monday. Oh sure, she'd been in a few relationships over the last ten years, but none of them meant diddly. In her heart of hearts, all along, though she might have divorced Jake, she knew—*knew*—he was the one and only man for her.

And now he was gone.

And Bonnie was gone.

And for all practical purposes…Candy's future was gone.

"COME ON, SWEETIE," Jake crooned Sunday morning, jiggling Bonnie as he paced the cramped motel room. "You're gonna be all right. Here," he said, reaching for her bottle. "Are you hungry?"

Howling all the harder, she batted the formula away with such force it landed halfway across the room to roll beneath the bed.

Great. Candy, aka Germ Police, would have a fit.

Correction, she *would have* had a fit. But seeing how she was no longer in either his or Bonnie's life, then he guessed she wouldn't have a say in the matter.

And the very idea made him want to puke.

Bonnie wailed on.

"Please, sweetie. Daddy's got a headache this

morning from trying to think of a way for us to fight your nasty old Aunt Elizabeth, and I really need you to be good.''

Bonnie cried on and off all night, but that morning her cries had become alarmingly intense, like the ones she'd cried just after Cal and Jenny passed away. But for the life of him, Jake couldn't figure why the munchkin would be crying like that now. He'd changed her diaper, fed her, checked her for fever.

Teething.

Yeah, she must be teething.

Cradling her in the crook of his left arm, he squirreled through her diaper bag with his free hand, digging, digging for her teething medicine, but it wasn't there.

Dammit. Though he'd been hasty in moving their gear out of Candy's, he was pretty sure he'd also been thorough. He gave the bag one more check—just to be sure—but came up empty-handed. He did find her favorite teething frog, so he handed her that just to see if it would help.

For an instant the baby quieted, giving the toy a tentative nibble, but ultimately she swatted it, like the bottle, under the bed and began wailing all the harder.

Perching on the edge of the bed, Jake did the only thing he knew in holding Bonnie close.

All the baby books said kids were pretty keen on picking up on their parent's vibes. Could she sense what a bad turn their lives had taken?

Cupping his big hand to the curve of her tiny head, for the millionth time he replayed the previous night's catastrophe.

What could he have done to make things turn out different? Sure, he supposed he could have lied to Candy, telling her that he'd like nothing better than to start all over again with her. But once Bonnie's adoption was finalized, what good would that have done except cause more pain?

"Oh, baby," he crooned over her exhausted sniffles. "I wish you could tell me what you think I should have done. I'm so damned afraid that had I agreed to all of Candy's hopes and dreams for our shared future, that in the end, all of us would have ended up hurt."

Bonnie's tear-dampened cheeks felt chilled, so he reached beside him for her favorite flannel blanket. The mere act of lifting it released precious fragrant memories. Sweet scents of Candy and her always-present chocolate perfume. Memories of watching her tuck that blanket around Bonnie's sturdy limbs, rocking her to sleep in the rocker he'd built for the express purpose of lulling his children off to dreamland.

Bonnie sighed against the blanket's fuzzy warmth. For the first time since their return to the sterile motel, she slept, fisting wads of the blanket in her chubby fingers, holding yet another piece of it over her nose. Gazing at her, she called to mind his own reaction just a few seconds earlier. If Jake didn't know better, he'd say she was breathing in the scent of Candy, reminding herself how loved she'd felt in Candy's arms.

The very implication was too much for Jake to bear. Surely, Bonnie couldn't have become attached to Candy in just a week? Attached to the point that she howled from missing her?

He didn't know much about babies, but what little he did know told him that, logically, Bonnie wasn't anywhere near mature enough to miss someone when they were gone. But then she'd sure missed her parents. Who was he to say she hadn't already formed a bond to the only other mother she'd known—Candy.

"Bonnie," he whispered, stroking her fine brows. "As much as I hate doing this. For your sake, we've got to go back into the lion's den. We've got to convince Candy to stay with us just a little while longer. Just long enough to get you legally mine, then wean you from her many charms."

And while we're at it, maybe we can wean me from Candy, too.

AFTER SPENDING HER NIGHT tossing and turning on Jake's recliner, inhaling his masculine essence, playing a game of hide-and-seek with his remembered warmth, Candy thought surely she must be having a nightmare for the doorbell to be ringing so bright and early Sunday morning.

But then there was also an insistent banging.

And then, "Come on, Candy, open up! I know you're in there and last night, on my way out the door, I left my key on the entry hall table."

Thank goodness for small favors!

"I'm coming, I'm coming," she said, tugging her rumpled evening gown down past her hips. Jake's emeralds still hugged her throat. If she hadn't planned to sell the exquisite necklace to contribute to Bonnie's college fund, she'd have ripped it from around her neck to throw it at the creep.

Yanking open the door, it was on the tip of her tongue to demand he turn right back around and leave when Bonnie grinned in his arms. The infant held out her chubby hands, pinching her fingers to show her desire for Candy to hold her.

"Why are you doing this, Jake?" She took Bonnie from him, squeezing the baby probably a little too close, but she didn't care. If this was the last time she saw Bonnie, she wanted to drink her in from the top of her down-covered head to the tips of her pink toes.

"Can I at least come in?"

"I'd rather you didn't."

He laughed. "I gathered that from the way you're blocking the door."

Candy looked to the ceiling and sighed. Unlike her, he'd changed out of his reunion finery and into a pair of khaki shorts and a white Key West Charlie's T-shirt. On his feet—deck shoes, no socks. His hair, as usual, was an adorably mussed mess. Candy wanted to think him ugly, but how could she gazing into those deep brown eyes? How many times had that dear chiseled face with just a mere look stroked her to rapturous pleasure?

More to the point this morning, how many times had that same handsome mug brought her to heart-rending pain?

Against her better judgment Candy stepped aside, waving him in.

Eyeing her before heading to his recliner, he said, "I see you got as much sleep as I did."

"Thanks. Glad to know you still find me attractive—not attractive enough to marry, though, right?"

He worked his jaw. "I didn't come here to fight, Candy Cane."

Hugging Bonnie close, Candy said, "Don't you *ever* call me that again."

"Sorry. It slipped out."

"Well it shouldn't have."

"Point taken. Now, if you don't mind, I have some things to say."

"No one's stopping you." Candy hated her snippy tone, but the whole instinctive fight-or-flight thing was funny. At that moment, she wasn't sure whether to take Bonnie and run, or to stay and fight Jake until he saw what an amazing gift he'd thrown away.

The gift of their newborn love.

Once again sighing, he said, "I guess there's no easy way to say this where I don't come off sounding like the world's biggest jerk, but here goes. I still want us to be married, Candy. The ugly things we said last night don't change my reasons for being here. In the eyes of the court, Bonnie needs a mother. I need a wife. If I don't get a wife, sixty-something spinster, Elizabeth Mannford, will get the baby she's always wanted." Leaning forward, hands on his knees, he said, "Marry me, Candy. *Please.* I'm not asking, I'm begging."

Still clutching Bonnie to her chest, Candy paced. Breakfront to the fireplace. Fireplace to breakfront. "Do you have any idea how ludicrous that sounds in light of the fact that less than twenty-four hours ago

I pledged myself to you *and* Bonnie heart and soul for the rest of my life?''

"I know," he said, sheepishly eyeing the floor.

"No, I think you don't know. The courage it took for me to overcome my fears was more than I ever imagined finding. But I did it. I did it, and I'm darned proud of the fact. As for you, all week you sat in that chair preaching to me about how all my fears were in my head. If only I would be logical, I'd see that they were just figments of my overworked imagination. Well, how about tasting a little of your own medicine, Jake? How about realizing that the past is in the past. I'm sorry if I hurt you. You hurt me. I thought we'd mutually agreed to call our past even, but by your admission of not loving me, of not being able to trust me, you've as much as said that in your mind, other than as a means for you to keep Bonnie, you want nothing more to do with me."

Jake tried storming to his feet, but the recliner's butt-hugging suction powers held him down. He looked ridiculous wrestling his way up and Candy was glad. He was too darned handsome for his own good and he deserved to be taken down a notch— even if it was just in his precious pride.

"Dammit," he growled. Finally free, he gave the thing a good, hard kick. "Stupid piece of—"

"Language," Candy warned, unable to hide her grin.

"This isn't funny."

"Sure it is, if you've got my view."

"Great," he said, rolling his eyes. "So not only

am I the bad guy, I'm generously providing you with comic relief. Glad I could be of service.''

"Me, too—for once.''

"Seriously, Candy, I'm in dire straights here. If I show up in Palm Breeze without a wife, my hopes of getting Bonnie are squashed.''

"Seriously, Jake, I realize that, which is partially why I already agreed to marry you. You're the one who threw my offer of a lifetime commitment back in my face.''

"And we both know why. Because I already made a lifetime commitment to you that after only five years into our 'till death do us part,' you threw back in my face.''

"Argh!'' she said, tossing up her free hand. "How many times do I have to tell you I fully admit to not thinking clearly back then? But you, Jake, you changed all of that. You made me see how precious love is, and how it'd be a crying shame to throw away what we share all because of a fear of what may or may not come out of the closet.''

Her tone softened, she paused to wipe a tear from her cheek before kissing Bonnie on her forehead. "You say you don't—or rather, can't—trust me. You say your fix to that is finding not a real wife, but a temporary one. Well, I say that's ridiculous. I say that goes against the grain of every wonderful thing you've taught me.''

"Candy, I—''

"No, let me finish. I fell asleep last night once again blaming my mother for our problems. But the truth is, her spirit has nothing to do with this.''

''Bull. All you have to do is say the word and we could be married by this afternoon.''

''Whoop-de-do. All this week, you've shown me glimpses into a fairy-tale realm where I don't just get the man I love, but a beautiful baby and the chance to create more beautiful babies. Monday, no matter how badly—how desperately—I wanted that very thing down deep in my heart, I never in a million years would have admitted it. At the reunion, I not only admitted it, but I asked you to create that magic with me for the rest of our lives.''

Tipping her chin up a notch, silent tears streaming down her cheeks, she courageously handed over Bonnie. ''I'm sorry,'' she said. ''But if I've learned anything over the past week, it's that I'm worth more than just a temporary husband. I want or all nothing. And if you're unable—or unwilling—to trust me not to break your heart, then that's your problem, not mine. As for Bonnie, you might be a lousy soul mate to me, but you're a great dad. When the time comes, I'll testify to that fact on a stack of bibles.''

His expression one of wounded incredulity, he shook his head. ''So that's it? I support you through your fears and you tell me mine are unfounded and stupid?''

''I never said that.''

''You didn't have to, it's written all over your face.'' Turning his back to her, he headed for the door.

Bonnie peered over his shoulder, holding out her arms and pinching her fingers.

"Goodbye, Candy. As is usually the case with you, it's been real."

Hugging herself, watching him and the most adorable baby in the whole wide world walk out the door and out of her life, Candy was certain the crushing pain in her chest was heart related. Maybe not in the traditional sense, but make no mistake, while she might not be having a technical heart attack, her heart was breaking.

Once before she'd watched this man walk out that door. Then, with the help of her grandfather and good friends, she'd survived. But now, Grandpa was gone. And first thing Monday morning, her family at Candy Kisses would be gone, as would every friend she'd ever made in Lonesome.

From the moment she stepped onto that plane headed to Peru, she'd be completely alone in the world.

For the first time in her life she'd been within inches of living a life she hadn't dared dream. For the first time in her life, she'd been truly happy.

At peace.

And she'd liked it. Oh, how she'd liked it.

And now, that part of her life was over.

Just as learning of her mother's death signified the end of one chapter, this final breakup with Jake signified another. Only instead of fighting to come out swinging at another day, she just felt tired.

She needed to pack.

Clean out the fridge and cupboards.

She needed to, but mentally couldn't. She lugged her emotionally beaten and battered body up the stairs and crawled into bed. The packing could be done later. Right now she needed healing sleep.

Chapter Fifteen

After leaving Candy's, Jake thought about crashing Warren and Franny's family breakfast, but realized that after eating, they'd be getting ready for church and he'd only be in the way.

Changing course, he aimed his white rental toward Dietz's apartment.

"Yeah," he said to the fitful munchkin in the back seat. "We'll go see Dietz. He's a man's man. If anyone'll understand and support my decision, it'll be my good friend Dietz."

Five minutes later Jake, Bonnie in his arms, climbed the rickety steps to Dietz's garage apartment.

He frowned.

The guy earned over sixty grand a year at the store, so what was he doing living in a dive like this?

Putting the thought to the back of his mind, Jake rapped three times on the wood-framed screen door.

From inside came the muffled sound of a curse, then a crash and breaking of glass. Out came another curse, a woman's giggle, then the sound of Dietz's heavy footsteps crossing the living room floor.

"Who is it?" Dietz growled.

"It's me, man. Jake. But I hear you've got company, so I'll catch you later."

"Forget about it," Dietz said, jerking open the door. "If this has something to do with Candy, Kel won't care."

"You spent the night with Kelly?"

Dietz shrugged.

Kelly, tugging at the hem of Dietz's ragtag Lonesome High football jersey, stepped up behind Dietz and slipped her arm around his waist. "This isn't what it looks like," she said. "I've been helping Dietz with his tax extension."

"Yeah," Dietz echoed. "Taxes. Extensions. Lots and *lots* of extensions."

"Oh, well…"

Dietz stepped aside, inviting Jake in.

With the shades drawn, shadows filled the overheated room. Dust motes danced in sunlight shafting past metal blinds. The air smelled stale—of an all-night party.

Jake aimed for the couch, but the navy-plaid cushions were littered with clothes. What he assumed to be Kelly's bra hung from the corner of the curtain rod. Her panties hugged the lip of an empty champagne bottle. Her red-sequined reunion gown lay puddled at his feet.

Neatly sidestepping it to turn back to the door, he said, "I should get going. Sorry to bust in on you two during all this paperwork. I just wanted to say goodbye."

"You're leaving?" Kelly said. "But I thought you and Candy would get back togeth—"

"You thought wrong," Jake said, lips pressed tight. "I was just over there and things got ugly."

"Which they wouldn't have if you two didn't love each other so much."

"With all due respect, stay out of this, Kel."

Her mock salute and condemning stare did nothing to soothe Jake's nerves. Dammit, he'd come here with the intention of having Dietz tell him he'd done the right thing. But now he was more convinced than ever that A, he'd done the right thing in leaving Candy. And B, he'd done the wrong thing in coming here.

"You're really leaving this time, huh?" Dietz rested his arm atop Kelly's shoulders.

"Yup. So now that I've said goodbye, I'll just be on my way."

Kelly stepped forward. Grasped his free hand. "Don't do this, Jake. Candy loves you and Bonnie. I know she does. She told me all that nonsense you spewed about feeling like you can't trust her, but you can. I promise."

He snorted. "That's great, Kel. So what are you gonna do when she asks for another divorce? Offer to marry me in her place?"

"Watch it," Dietz warned. "You're like a brother to me, man, but there's no need for you to vent on Kelly. She didn't do anything wrong." A sharp laugh passed his lips. "In fact, if anyone around here is to blame, it's you."

JAKE HAD HAD ENOUGH of small-town life, which was why he'd called his pilot right after leaving Dietz's.

Problem was, the jet was socked in by Seattle fog that wasn't expected to lift anytime soon. Which was why Jake was now trapped. Here he was at 2:00 a.m., once again lying on his lumpy Oak Lodge bed, staring at the equally lumpy popcorn ceiling.

Bonnie slept fitfully in her crib. Maybe not as unaware as he'd like of the courtroom battle to come.

That afternoon, he'd killed time by hiking.

He'd fitted Bonnie into her baby backpack and marched through miles and miles of forest. Hoping by pushing his body, his mind could make sense of the recent chain of events.

Candy claimed to love him, but if she really loved him, they'd be married. He'd helped her deal with her issues about her mother, so why couldn't she understand that, evidently, he had a few issues all his own?

Issues that started by wondering why she'd left him in the first place.

Get a grip, man. She went all over that. Because she was afraid to have kids, remember?

Okay, she claimed that was the reason, but what if it had been about something more? Maybe she hated that slight crook in his nose or thought he had bad breath? Maybe she'd been sick of him leaving his clothes all over the floor or not doing enough dishes?

Maybe it was the fact that instead of listening to her fears, you went on and on about your own desires. You wanted kids so bad you never even stopped to ask why she didn't. Face it, man, you were an insensitive jerk even back then.

Jake worked his jaw.

An insensitive jerk?

That was harsh—even for his own conscience.

Yeah, but could it be true?

He raked his fingers through his hair. How was he supposed to know what was true? What was real? He thought what they had shared the first time around had been real, but look where that had ended up.

How could he have fallen so hard for Candy, so fast, all over again?

All week he'd told himself his rushes of affection for her—not to mention, passion—were just passing things. Poignant souvenirs from their past. But what if all of it was more? What if far from his claim to not love her, he did? What if maybe he'd never even fallen out of love?

What if in being too damned afraid to trust, he threw away the best thing he'd ever had?

Even worse, what if he did trust, only to once again be made the fool?

UNABLE TO SLEEP, Candy had pulled an all-nighter, feverishly packing clothes and supplies. Monday morning, she looked and felt like any number of four-letter words, and even though it was an overcast day, slipped on sunglasses for her short trek to Kelly's.

"What are you doing here?" Kelly asked upon answering her door.

"Nice to see you, too," Candy said, barging past

her friend who was dressed in a robe and hot rollers. "I figured you'd want all of this food Jake bought."

"Anything good?" She picked at one of the bags.

On her way to the kitchen, Candy shrugged. "Sorry, but I ate all the Nutter Butter and Oreo. There are a few bags of Fritos, though, and more cans of chili than any sane person could eat in a lifetime."

"Keep those. They won't ruin."

"Ha," Candy said, setting the bags on Kelly's white-tiled counter, then stashing various items in the cupboards, pantry or fridge. "Everything that reminds me of that creep is ruined."

"You don't mean that." Kelly hefted herself onto the counter. "I told you how awful he looked the morning after your fight."

"Yeah," Candy said, can of chili in hand. "Let's go over that morning again. What exactly were you doing with Dietz?"

Kelly rolled her eyes. "I already told you, he needed help with his taxes—and don't try changing the subject."

"I'm not. I just think that since the subject of me and Jake is played out, we might as well focus on you."

AN HOUR LATER, on the way to Candy Kisses' closing, Candy had to pull over on quiet Elmdale Lane because the crushing pain of losing her shop and Jake and Bonnie brought on yet another river of tears.

Jeez. She'd thought once she'd calmed herself with a pep talk on how much fun her trip was going to be, she'd feel better. After all, how many tears could one girl cry?

How many times could one heart stumble over the same man?

Reapplying mascara with the help of the rearview mirror, she reasoned that her biggest mistake had been in ever thinking she was well and truly over him. Deep down, she'd known after being with him only five minutes that not only did she still love him, but that she'd always love him.

No amount of trips would ease that pain.

But then, neither would losing herself in her work. Past experience had taught her that.

So what was there left to do? Join the Peace Corps? The army? Maybe a nice, quiet convent?

Resolutely shifting her van into drive, she steeled her shoulders. She'd been fine before Jake blasted back into her life and she'd be fine again.

Soon. Just any second.

Just as soon as she'd cried one last batch of tears.

Easing the van back into park, Candy fished through her purse for a tissue. Looked as though it was going to be a long day.

CANDY LEFT the closing with an odd mixture of relief and regret. Guess the only way she'd find out if she'd done the right thing was in letting the future play out. One thing was for sure, she—

A white sedan careened sideways into three parking spaces while the driver hopped out, dashed to the back door to reach for an achingly familiar pink bundle, then made another mad dash to where Candy stood gaping on the Green Country Title Office's front walk.

"Are we too late?" Jake shouted midway across the lot. "You didn't do it yet, did you? Please tell me you didn't sell Candy Kisses."

By this time Jake and Bonnie had reached her. The painful pleasure of seeing them again brought on a fresh batch of tears, especially when Bonnie bucked against Jake, chubby fingers pinching for Candy to take her into her arms.

When Candy did, Jake, still breathing hard, said, "She missed you."

"How do you know?"

He shrugged. "I just do. She's been cranky as hell. I'm assuming about not getting her way."

"About what?"

"Tell me first. Candy Kisses. Is it gone?"

Candy swallowed hard. "Why do you care?"

After flashing her the same lopsided grin that had melted her back in the summer before fourth grade, only to gain potency every year since, he said, "Simple. I love you. And because if you put one half the love into our marriage and raising Bonnie as you've put into making Candy Kisses the most favored shop in town, there's no way we can fail."

Candy's heart lurched.

"Marry me, Candy. Not for Bonnie's sake, but for me…for you. I—I'm sorry about what I said at the reunion. I was afraid to trust—to hope—you'd fallen as hard for me as I had for you. But now I see what a fool I've been. Not just to give you up ten years ago, but again Saturday night.''

''I can't believe this is happening,'' Candy said with a teary sniffle.

''What, Candy Cane? That as usual I'm a day late and dollar short? I'm sorry I didn't get here in time to stop you from selling.'' Reaching into his back pocket for his wallet, he said, ''Look, if you promise to stop crying, I'll buy back Candy Kisses.'' He fanned a half dozen gold cards. ''I'll double what the Hammonds paid, only please stop crying and giving me that look you know I've never been able to read.''

''I-if you'd just hush already, I'll tell you what this look means. I didn't sell, Jake. I took a gamble—well, several actually. And when you drove up, I was just debating whether I'd done the right or wrong thing.''

''Tell me what you did and I'll let you know.''

Hugging Bonnie, she said, ''I changed my flight plans.''

''Huh? You didn't sell, but you're still leaving?''

She laughed. ''Don't you see? I hired the Hammonds to manage Candy Kisses, but they won't be buying it since I decided I couldn't go through with the sale. Not so much for me, but for Bonnie, because every little girl should have her own candy shop. I changed my flight plans to swing by Palm Breeze. I thought you'd already left, so I was for once following Kelly's advice by going down there to get you.''

Cinching Candy close, with cooing Bonnie sandwiched between, Jake said, "You were, huh? What if I still hadn't come to my senses?"

"Simple. I planned on using a little reverse psychology. This guy I know—you might know him, too, goes by the name of Dietz—anyway, he says the sure-fire way to get a man is to tell him he wants one thing, all the while, making him truly desire something else—like me." On her tiptoes, Candy leaned up and over Bonnie to seal her speech with a kiss.

She'd meant for it to be a simple kiss. One of promise and hope, but it was Jake who took it to a whole other level.

It was Jake whose lips spoke more eloquently than words ever could, murmuring such implied phrases as, *We'll be together forever* and *Whose laugh do you think our kids'll have—yours or mine?*

"I love you," Jake said.

"I love you," Candy replied.

"So?" Jake pulled away, rubbing his hands together. "How fast can we pull this wedding of yours together? I'm thinking I'll fly in fancy-schmancy caterers and floral designers from Palm Breeze. We'll rent a few humongous tents in Springfield. Think they'd have any harpists or string players for hire?"

"Slow down," Candy said. "I don't need any of that."

"The hell you don't. I almost lost you once and this time I want the whole world to know you're mine."

"Really, Jake, it doesn't—"

He quieted her protests with a kiss. A mind-shattering, earth-rocking kiss that quivered her knees, curled her toes and, in general, made her want whatever Jake wanted—to a point.

"Okay," she said. "Bonnie and I will go along with throwing the biggest, flashiest, most romantic wedding this town has ever seen on one condition."

"What's that?"

"After the wedding…"

"Yeah?"

"And after the honeymoon…"

"Yeah?"

"No more chili for breakfast!"

Epilogue

"Am I doing this right?" Candy asked Jake under her breath. Eight months pregnant, she was having a tough time wielding the giant gold scissors Palm Breeze's mayor had presented her with to cut the second Candy Kisses store's big, pink ribbon.

One hand around her waist, the other holding Bonnie, who had long since officially been declared his—and of course, Candy's—Jake whispered in her ear, "Sweetie, as hot as you look in that pink dress, this crowd wouldn't care if you stood on your head to cut the ribbon."

"Hot? Are you kidding me? I must've gained like fifty pounds since our wedding."

"Mmm," he crooned, kissing her neck. "And I adore each and every one of them."

Stepping back from the microphone, the mayor cleared his throat. "Uh, while it's always a pleasure to see two young people so obviously in love, I do have a grade school groundbreaking ceremony later this afternoon."

Jake drank in the sight of his wife's cheeks blushing the pink of her dress. God, how he loved her. "Sorry," he said to the mayor. "I just can't keep my hands off of her."

"Perfectly understandable," the mayor said with a bold wink.

Jake stepped back and watched the business woman he'd always known Candy could be emerge. While it had been his idea to open a second Candy Kisses smack-dab in the center of his Palm Breeze Galaxy Sports superstore, from the idea all the way to its inception, she'd taken charge.

Each new day together brought new surprises. She made leaps in confidence. He made leaps in humility.

Together, they leaped in trust.

Candy cut the ribbon while simultaneously a local high school band launched into a blaring rendition of "The Candy Man." Wearing a smile so big it hurt, she stepped over the fallen ribbon and behind the glowing oak-and-marble counter—thoughtfully reproduced from the original Candy Kisses. "May I help you?" she asked the mayor's wife, her first official customer.

"I'll take a Coco Loco and three Bonnie Blues."

"You got it," Candy said, hustling to fill the woman's order.

Inside Candy, the baby kicked, and in that second, as never before, she had one of those crystalline moments where time stood still.

What she had finally found, not just in that instant, but forever, was perfection.

Just to the right of the counter stood handsome Jake, an adorable Bonnie grinning in his arms. As a surprise, Jake had flown in many of their Lonesome friends. Kelly and Dietz, who still claimed to not be a couple even though they now did taxes on a regular basis. Warren and Franny and all of their brood. Rick was still on his own, but if Candy had her way, he wouldn't be for long. Mrs. Starling and Elizabeth Mannford stood beaming beside an actor dressed as an ice cream cone. Both women had become grandmotherly fixtures in the Peterson home, especially Elizabeth who had confessed to wanting Bonnie so badly because of how badly she missed her family. Well, once Jake and Candy had heard that, they'd welcomed her with loving arms into their newly forged family. Even the loving spirits of family long gone to heaven but always near in memory felt especially close on this magical day.

Even beyond being excited about her business expansion, beyond her excited anticipation over becoming a mommy to a second beautiful baby, Candy rejoiced in a deeper, quiet, more profoundly moving sense of excitement. The one that accompanied her every thought of Jake.

She was in love.

Gloriously, wondrously, crazily in love. Forever in love. Dizzily in—

"Uh, Candy?" Jake said, stealing up behind her. "My manager just gave me the heads up on a delivery that's blocking the front door."

"What kind of delivery?" she asked, handing the mayor a strawberry-cheesecake ice cream cone.

"A very special delivery," Kelly said, stepping up

to the counter. "The kind that deals in revenge that's been a long time coming."

Eyebrows furrowed, Candy turned the serving operations over to three new employees, then followed her grinning friend. Weaving through the crowd, she asked Jake, "Do you have any idea what she's talking about?"

Arm around her waist, he said, "Not a clue."

Minutes later, Candy hedged past throngs of chuckling customers only to have her cheeks burn flamingo pink.

"Kelly Foster," she said, hands on her hips, "hauling that musty old thing all the way to Florida isn't very funny."

"Funny, hmm…" Kelly said, taking Dietz's hand. "Interesting choice in words. Especially since that's what a couple fishermen thought about the sight of you and Jake going at it on that couch one sunny day last spring."

While Candy wished the floor would open up, swallowing her, the old gold couch and the huge glittering sign proclaiming Goldilocks to be the Official Love Couch of The True King And Queen Of Lonesome High's Class Of 1987, Jake that no-good husband of hers actually laughed, slapping Kelly and Dietz high-fives.

"Good one," he said with a wide grin, scooping Candy into his arms. "And it's going to be even better once we try this old thing out."

"Jake!" Candy squealed.

"Candy!" her husband teased, easing her onto the very cushions where— Never mind. This was just too horrible. The couch. The deeds. The fact that fishermen had witnessed those deeds!

Lowering himself on of top her, to the sound of thundering applause, wolf whistles and cheers, Candy tried putting up a good fight, but in the end, realized the futility of her struggles. The fact of the matter was that she not only loved this old couch, but this not-so-old man and every single even slightly wanton act they'd ever shared.

"Jake?" she asked during a brief break from kissing for air.

"Yeah?"

"How fast do you think we can have Goldilocks delivered to our bedroom?"

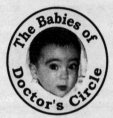
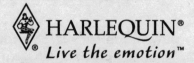

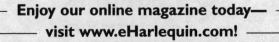

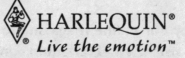

celebrates its 20th Anniversary

This June, we have a distinctive lineup that features
another wonderful title in

The Deveraux Legacy

series from bestselling author

CATHY GILLEN THACKER
Taking Over the Tycoon
(HAR #973)

Sexy millionaire Connor Templeton is used to
getting whatever—whomever—he wants!
But has he finally met his match in
one beguiling single mother?

And on sale in July 2003,
Harlequin American Romance premieres
a brand-new miniseries,
Cowboys by the Dozen,
from **Tina Leonard.**

Available at your favorite retail outlet.

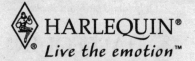

Visit us at www.eHarlequin.com

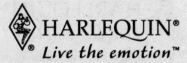